"I'm catching that garter," Kyle declared. "Stand back."

The crowd started at ten and began to count backward. At *eight,* Kyle studied his competition.

At *five,* he positioned himself front and center.

At *three,* he placed his hands on his knees.

At *two,* he imagined sliding that garter up Clarissa Cohagan's shapely leg.

"One."

The bit of white lace and satin soared through the air. Kyle raced ahead of the others and snatched the garter in midflight. Someone tackled him from behind, but when all was said and done, the garter was held tight in the fist of his right hand.

Raising his hand above his head, he straightened his arm and shouted, *"Yes!"*

Dear Reader,

This month, Silhouette Romance presents an exciting new FABULOUS FATHER from Val Whisenand. Clay Ellis is *A Father Betrayed*—surprised to learn he has a child and has been deceived by the woman he'd always loved.

Long Lost Husband is a dramatic new romance from favorite author Joleen Daniels. Andrea Ballanger thought her ex-husband, Travis Hunter, had been killed in the line of duty. But then she learned Travis was very much alive....

Bachelor at the Wedding continues Sandra Steffen's heartwarming WEDDING WAGER series about three brothers who vow they'll never say "I do." This month, Kyle Harris loses the bet—and his heart—when he catches the wedding garter and falls for would-be bride Clarissa Cohagan.

Rounding out the month, you'll find love and laughter as a determined single mom tries to make herself over completely—much to the dismay of the man who loves her—in Terry Essig's *Hardheaded Woman*. In *The Baby Wish*, Myrna Mackenzie tells the touching story of a woman who longs to be a mother. Too bad her handsome boss has given up on family life—or so he thought.

And visit Sterling, Montana, for a delightful tale from Kara Larkin. There's a new doctor in town, and though he isn't planning on staying, pretty Deborah Pingree hopes he'll make some *Home Ties*.

Until next month, happy reading!

Anne Canadeo
Senior Editor
Silhouette Romance

Please address questions and book requests to:
Silhouette Reader Service
U.S.: 3010 Walden Ave., P.O. Box 1325, Buffalo, NY 14269
Canadian: P.O. Box 609, Fort Erie, Ont. L2A 5X3

BACHELOR AT THE WEDDING

Sandra Steffen

Published by Silhouette Books
America's Publisher of Contemporary Romance

For my editor, Melissa Jeglinski,
who helps keep the magic and the fun in writing.

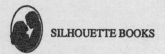

SILHOUETTE BOOKS

ISBN 0-373-19045-X

BACHELOR AT THE WEDDING

Copyright © 1994 by Sandra E. Steffen

SANDRA STEFFEN

Creating memorable characters is one of Sandra's favorite aspects of writing. She's always been a romantic, and is thrilled to be able to spend her days doing what she loves—bringing her characters to life on her computer screen.

Sandra grew up in Michigan, the fourth of ten children, all of whom have taken the old adage "Go forth and multiply" quite literally. Add to this her husband, who is her real-life hero, their four school-age sons, who keep their lives in constant motion, their gigantic cat, Percy, and Sandra's wonderful friends, in-laws and neighbors, and what do you get? Chaos, of course, but also a wonderful sense of belonging she wouldn't trade for the world.

We, the undersigned, do hereby declare our state of bachelorhood to be a sacred trust. We shall in no way attempt to endanger our single status by dating seriously, fathering a child or—heaven forbid—falling in love. He who does not abide by this contract shall be banished from the brotherhood of bachelors for all time.

This contract we do honor. Let no woman place a ring upon our finger.

Mitch Harris

Kyle Harris

Taylor Harris

Chapter One

He'd been told his deep voice contained a tinge of wonder and the kind of warmth that called to mind moonlit nights and rumpled sheets. Kyle was familiar with both, and as he spoke into the microphone, neither were far from his mind. All because of one woman, one woman who wouldn't even meet his eyes.

"For those of you who don't know me, I'm Kyle Harris. And no, it isn't a coincidence that Mitch and I have the same last name. Our parents planned it that way."

He waited a moment for the guests to quiet. "Before the happy couple leaves for their honeymoon, Raine would like to throw her bouquet."

He smiled his most beguiling grin as everyone in the crowd turned toward him. Everyone except the woman, that is. From across the room his gaze followed the delicate line of that woman's profile. When he spoke again, his voice was lower, huskier. She was getting to him, and she didn't even appear to be trying.

"Now we're going to have a little fun, so I'd like every *single* woman from seventeen to ninety-three to gather 'round.'' Kyle watched as some of Mitch and Raine's female friends and relatives slowly made their way to the center of the floor. His pulse rate quickened as the woman across the room stood.

So, she's single.

Instead of stepping onto the dance floor, she turned her back to him and made her way toward the far side of the room where the caterers were preparing to leave. For some reason, he was disappointed. Not that he minded the view. Her royal blue suit was tight in all the right places. A wide belt cinched in her waist and the slit in the back of the skirt stopped just short of being provocative. But Kyle had always preferred a woman to walk toward him.

He lured the remaining single women onto the dance floor, but his thoughts were on the one at the other side of the room. As he waited for his spiky-haired second cousin to stand and thread her way toward the other women waiting in the center of the dance floor, his gaze settled on the woman he couldn't stop thinking about.

He'd seen her for the first time hours ago when he and his brothers were waiting for the wedding to begin. Mitch had been telling them about the "something new," a skimpy bit of lace and satin he'd given Raine to wear beneath her wedding gown. Taylor had slapped Mitch on the back and Mitch had grinned, a smug smile on his lips, lips that used to utter more detailed intimacies about the women he dated but were sealed since meeting Raine. Taylor had murmured a choice word or two but Kyle barely noticed, because, at that moment, the door to the pastor's study had opened from the hall, and *she* had walked in.

"Guys, this is Clarissa Cohagan," Mitch had murmured. "My brothers, Kyle and Taylor."

She'd acknowledged the introductions with the briefest of smiles, her gaze lingering on Kyle's for only a moment before saying, "The reverend is ready for the three of you up front."

Kyle didn't have long to gaze from her dark hair to the high heels of her royal blue shoes before the door had swished shut behind her. But he'd heard the soft rustle of her skirt as it slipped over her thighs and whatever she was—or wasn't—wearing underneath. He couldn't remember the last time he'd reacted so strongly and so immediately to the sight of a beautiful woman.

She hadn't said another word. And she hadn't met his look since. Not during the candlelight ceremony or throughout the entire reception. But she would. He'd make sure of that.

When all the unmarried female wedding guests were assembled on the dance floor, Kyle murmured, "Okay, Raine. Turn around."

His new sister-in-law turned to face him, and Kyle understood what his brother saw in Raine McAlister, Raine Harris now. She was blond and slender and full of spark. But Kyle hadn't fantasized even once about what *Raine* was wearing beneath her dress.

At the other end of the room, Clarissa Cohagan began to wend her way through the crowd. The way her skirt smoothed over *her* thighs had his imagination doing the lambada.

"One."

Kyle watched as she sidestepped a rambunctious child.

"Two."

Skirting the edge of the dance floor, Clarissa picked her way past more spectators.

"Three."

Raine tossed the bouquet over her left shoulder, sending the flowers sailing high above the raised hands of the women on the floor. Out of sheer instinct and split-second reflexes, Clarissa threw her hands up to protect her face. And caught the bouquet.

Kyle didn't think he'd forget the look that settled on her face as she realized what she'd done. Light from the overhead fixtures danced in her dark eyes. Her bearing was almost stiff, but proud, even in such chaotic circumstances.

Raine laughed then ran to hug her friend. The guests clapped and Raine's younger brother shouted, "All those years of coaching Little League paid off, didn't they, Rainie?"

The guests laughed louder. "And now all you single guys!" Kyle murmured into the microphone. It didn't take any prodding to get the men out on the floor. They practically scrambled over one another to be the first one there.

Cousin Trudy taunted, "You aren't going to try, Kyle? Always a groomsman and never a groom."

Kyle handed the microphone to one of his married cousins, sputtering, "Just keep Trudy away from me." If anyone caught that garter, it was going to be him.

On his way past his brother, Kyle whispered, "I'll give you fifty bucks if you throw that garter to me."

Mitch chuckled wickedly. "You'll have to jump for it, fair and square. Besides, Taylor just offered me seventy-five."

A short, robust lady with silver curls blocked his path. "We're all rootin' for ya, Kyle. Just forget that you're the oldest one out there and reach for that garter!"

His voice was deceptively low as he answered. "At thirty-six I'm hardly over the hill, Aunt Millie. I'm catching that garter. Now stand back and give me some room."

For the single men, the crowd started at ten and began to count backward. At *eight* Kyle studied his competition. Taylor and Raine's brother, his most prominent opponents, were poised and ready.

At *five* he positioned himself front and center.

At *three* he placed his hands on his knees.

At *two* he took a deep breath and imagined sliding that garter up Clarissa Cohagan's shapely leg.

"One."

The bit of white lace and satin soared through the air like a dove in slow motion. Kyle raced ahead of the others and snatched the garter in midflight. Someone tackled him from behind, but when all was said and done, that garter was held tight in the fist of his right hand.

He stood up and made a show of brushing himself off. Raising his hand above his head, he straightened his arm and shouted, "Yes!"

The others grumbled and shook their heads as they sauntered back to the sidelines, leaving Kyle and Clarissa alone on the dance floor. A chair was brought out and what sounded like cheap striptease music played over the speakers. Kyle, in his glory, swaggered toward the woman waiting for him in the center of the floor. To those in the distance, she may have appeared to be enjoying herself. Her unease was evident only to him.

"Raine warned me."

"About me?" Kyle asked.

"About your family." She made a show of smiling for the guests.

"They're totally juvenile." He dipped his head near hers and was surprised at how short she was. Barefoot she wouldn't be more than five-three.

"They're expecting a show." She walked around the chair slowly and sat down. "Let's give them what they want."

Kyle's heart hammered in his chest. She'd surprised him. It had been a long time since he'd been surprised, even longer than it had been since he'd felt so overheated with so little provocation. He went down on one knee and watched as she crossed her legs. The guests hooted. One or two whistled. As far as Kyle was concerned, the crowd had disappeared.

He touched his fingers to her ankle then removed her high-heeled shoe, tossing it haphazardly over his shoulder. She uncrossed her legs, arched her right foot and pointed her toes.

Kyle kept his touch light and teasing, but his tux grew more uncomfortable by the second. Slowly he glided the garter over her ankle, up a shapely calf to her narrow knee. Her nylons were smooth as silk, the skin beneath his fingertips warm. He toyed with a sudden wish that his lips could follow the trail his hands had just taken.

"Higher. Higher. Higher." The guests wanted more.

He straightened his spine and looked up into her face. Her full lips wore a faint pout, but her eyes, the darkest brown he'd ever seen, didn't lie. She wasn't averse to his touch. He fleetingly wondered what her eyes would tell him if they were alone, instead of surrounded by a roomful of people.

With both hands, he slid the garter past her knee. The hem of her skirt hiked higher, exposing the lacy edge of her black slip. He'd wondered what she was wearing beneath her proper suit. Now he knew. Black lace.

Somewhere in the background, guests were clapping and hooting, but the blood rushing through Kyle's veins obliterated most of their noise. His instinctive response to this woman was powerful, and a wave of heat shimmered through him, blocking out all but desire, and the wish to explore where that desire would take them.

After several moments he realized his fingers were no longer touching her soft thigh. She'd taken both his hands in hers, effectively ending their little demonstration. "Show's over," she declared.

Kyle, for one, hated to see it end. His gaze climbed from her hands to her eyes, and back again. He retrieved Clarissa's shoe but when he moved to slide it onto her foot, she stiffened and took it from his hand. He let it go, but not before his fingers had skimmed her hand and slid over her wrist.

"Dance with me later?" he asked, lowering his voice to the tone reputed to sweep women off their feet.

"I don't think so, Kyle," she replied evenly.

Clarissa felt his interest. It was there in the touch of his fingers on her wrists, and deep in his eyes. She slid her foot into her shoe without taking her eyes from his. For a moment she'd actually enjoyed his touch. She wasn't planning to enjoy it again.

"If you'll excuse me..." She stood, turned and disappeared behind a group of guests standing near the punch bowl.

She checked on the punch and coffee, made certain the caterers had left everything in order, eyed the decorations, the leftover wedding cake, mentally checking off every single detail she'd seen to. After five years of owning and operating Weddings, Parties & More, it had become second nature. Having her heart climb to her throat when her gaze locked with a best man's wasn't.

She made her living planning weddings, from formal and dignified to small and spontaneous, and nearly everything in between. People were willing to pay an exorbitant fee for her thoroughness and eye for detail. She was good at what she did, and she was proud of it.

She automatically searched for her friend and assistant, Raine Harris, today's bride. In her ivory-colored floor-length wedding gown, Raine wasn't difficult to spot. Nor was her genuine happiness. The reason for that happiness was never far from her side, her new husband, Mitch Harris.

There was something about those Harris brothers. Raine was completely taken in by their laid-back charm. In every other way, her assistant was levelheaded, completely trustworthy. Clarissa *liked* Mitch, even went so far as indulging in Raine's head-in-the-clouds fervor for him. The verdict was still out on the other two brothers.

What she wouldn't indulge in was her own initial reaction to the oldest Harris brother. *Predatory male* might as well be stamped across his forehead. It was in his voice, in his eyes, in his smile. But if he was predatory, she was *off limits.* She'd taken herself out of that game over five years ago, and she didn't intend to reenlist.

What Clarissa needed to do was get her mind off Kyle Harris and on the duties at hand. She looked around the room, noticing the huge drops of rain pelting the high windows. With only one week until Christmas, she would have preferred fluffy white snow to set the holiday mood. She could plan a wedding down to the smallest detail, but the weather was one thing she couldn't change.

Five years ago she'd been told there was something else she couldn't change, but she'd go to her grave before she accepted that verdict. For now, she pushed the thought away and concentrated on the wedding reception and the water hitting the windowpanes. Her assistant loved the rain, claiming she'd fallen in love with Mitch during a summer shower, so it seemed only fitting that rain was forecast for the rest of the night.

At a decorated table nearby, Raine and Mitch, with the help of a few close friends, were opening their gifts. Clarissa stepped closer to watch. Mitch's brothers, Kyle and Taylor, needled and teased the wedding couple endlessly. The bride and groom seemed oblivious, exclaiming with equal delight over china and blenders, fine crystal and hand towels.

When Mitch reached for one box in particular, more guests crowded around. Clarissa stepped closer and watched as Mitch tore at the paper and lifted the lid, extracting what appeared to be an old bowling trophy.

Mitch held it up for the crowd to see and Kyle clasped his brother's shoulder. "You won it, Mitch, you old dog."

Their mother piped up and exclaimed, "That silly trophy. I should have thrown it out years ago when I had the chance. Imagine winning a trophy for dating an older girl or an astronaut, a Dallas Cowboys cheerleader or for being the first to marry!"

In a mock-solemn voice, Mitch said, "It's ours, Raine. Permanently."

"Don't be too hasty," Taylor grumbled. "Kyle and I will figure out a way to win it back, won't we, Kyle?"

The guests laughed uproariously, but Clarissa didn't find it funny. Raine had told her about that trophy, about how it had all started years ago when the three Harris brothers were thirteen, fourteen and fifteen respectively. It seems Taylor, the youngest, had wanted to ask an older girl out and the other two had bet him he wouldn't. Taylor had won that bet, and had been awarded his father's old bowling trophy as payment. After that, there always seemed to be a standing bet between them. Clarissa hadn't heard about the astronaut or Dallas cheerleader, but she did know that Mitch had won the latest bet when he'd been the first to marry.

"They look happy, don't they?"

She hadn't noticed Kyle's approach until his voice shimmered over her. She'd once read that his voice brought to mind sultry nights and long, slow kisses. Until now, she hadn't known what that particular reporter had meant. Kyle's job as disc jockey at a radio station along the outskirts of Philadelphia had made his voice one of the most sought after in eastern Pennsylvania. Now Clarissa understood why.

"I just hope she doesn't have her head in the clouds," she murmured, turning to glance up into blue eyes as alluring as his voice.

"You don't think they'll make it?"

Her gaze sought out the couple in question, who happened to look deliriously happy as they stole a quick kiss before tearing the paper from another gift. "I hope they do. But I'm afraid their chances aren't good. Statistics have proven it."

His silence drew her gaze. His look was incredulous. "You plan weddings for a living, yet you don't believe in the institution of marriage?"

A middle-aged man Raine had earlier introduced as Uncle Martin interrupted further conversation. He slapped Kyle on the back, exclaiming, "One Harris brother down, two to go, aye, boy?"

Clarissa looked up just in time to see Kyle scowl. He slipped his finger between his neck and the stiff collar of his starched shirt, and grumbled, "Whose idea was it to wear bow ties, anyway?"

His question didn't deter his uncle. Martin Harris turned to her and said, "Clara, isn't it?" Before she could correct him, he continued. "I understand you're to thank for planning this marvelous wedding."

"Raine and I planned it together...."

"And what a fine job you've done, too. I just love a good wedding. In fact, I don't mind telling you I'd like to see Kyle, here, married and happy, too."

"That's nice—"

Once again, the older Harris interrupted Clarissa's response. "Tell me, Clara, have you ever been married?"

Although she leveled her look at the older man, she didn't miss the curiosity in Kyle's expression. Honesty should put an end to his interest.

"Yes. Now, if you'll excuse me, it looks as if Raine and Mitch are preparing to leave." Clarissa cast a brief smile at both Harris men then turned and wound her way through the crowd toward Raine.

Kyle derived little satisfaction from leaning on Taylor's doorbell at eight-thirty the following morning. Only when the door was unlocked and thrown open did he remove his finger from the button.

"I should have known it was you. Don't you ever sleep?"

As the shaft of early-winter sunlight and cold air hit his brother's bare chest and eyes, Kyle's scowl deepened. "Your greeting leaves a lot to be desired, Tay. Besides, sleeping late is for old folks." He sauntered past Taylor, opened the blinds in his living room and began to fill the coffeemaker in his brother's small kitchen.

"What do you think you're doing?"

"Making coffee."

"You don't have a coffeemaker in *your* kitchen?"

"I don't have a basketball hoop."

Taylor rubbed his eyes and stretched. "It's cold and wet and you couldn't have had any more sleep than I have. What's up, Kyle?"

The coffeemaker hissed as the hot water began to drip through the grounds. "I'm restless. Let's play a round of one-on-one." Kyle watched as Taylor inspected two chipped mugs for possible use. Of the three Harris brothers, Taylor was definitely the most typical bachelor. Of course, Mitch wasn't a bachelor anymore.

"How can you be restless after all the dancing you did last night? You must have danced with every woman there."

Every woman except one.

Clarissa Cohagan had turned down his first invitation. He would have asked again, and again, but she'd told Uncle Martin she was married and Kyle had drawn the line at pursuing married women a long time ago, no matter how beautiful the woman, no matter how great the attraction.

Just because he hadn't pursued her didn't mean he hadn't watched her. She seldom sat down, and rarely smiled. When she did smile, he could have sworn it didn't reach her eyes, those big, brown, unfathomable eyes.

"It's hard to believe Mitch is really *married*," Taylor said, handing Kyle a mug of coffee.

Kyle stared into his coffee and mumbled, "Yeah." It was harder to believe Clarissa Cohagan was. She hadn't *seemed* married. But people didn't lie about something like that. He should have realized something was amiss by her reaction to catching the bouquet. Obviously a married woman wouldn't care to have a stranger put a garter on her leg.

"Wrapping up that old trophy was ingenious. The entire family said so. We have to come up with a new bet." Once Taylor woke up, he was a nonstop talker.

Kyle shook his head and sent his most hostile glare in his brother's direction. "Oh, no. I never agreed to a new bet. Leave me out of it."

"Come on, Kyle. We can't let Mitch keep the trophy.... I'll probably get hate mail from my neighbors for waking them up, but I say it's time for that brotherly little game of one-on-one you asked for...."

An hour later Kyle was stooped from overexertion. His hands were numb from the cold and his foot ached where Taylor had landed on it. He hated to admit it, but maybe Aunt Millie was right. Maybe he was getting old.

"All right, Kyle. My point. I win so the bet continues," Taylor bragged.

"This is ridiculous," Kyle protested loudly. He didn't care if he did wake up the neighbors. "Winning Dad's old bowling trophy for dating an older girl when we were teens was one thing, but Mitch outdid us both this time, Tay. He's not only married, but he's the first to have a kid, too. How are we ever going to top that?"

"Joey's a great kid, but Mitch didn't even know about him until three months ago, so the fact that our middle brother was the first to father a child doesn't count. We could always say the first to knowingly become a father of, say, three, wins the bet."

Kyle felt the blood drain from his head and felt his face turn pale. "How do you plan to do that?"

"There's the old adage—beg, borrow or steal. But I've always thought the old-fashioned way would be more fun." Taylor wiggled his eyebrows then tossed the ball to Kyle's numb hands.

"Forget it. I'm not participating in any more bets."

"Come on, Kyle. What's gotten in to you? I'm kidding about having kids. Becoming a father without becoming a husband isn't my style. But I'm not about to let Mitch keep that trophy. I've never known you to accept defeat. What's going on?"

For a moment Kyle stood looking at his younger brother. How many times had he heard an aunt or uncle or neighbor tell his parents they'd had triplets the hard way. One at a time. Even today, at thirty-four, thirty-five and thirty-six, people occasionally mistook them for triplets. Kyle had never seen it, but people claimed they all looked incredibly alike. The three brothers had the same build, the same large-boned frame and the same dark blue eyes. As far as Kyle was concerned, that's where the similarities ended. Mitch's hair was dark, Kyle's was sandy blond and Taylor's was somewhere in between.

Kyle dribbled the ball a few times, then eyed the basket and took a shot. The ball had swished through the net and bounced on the concrete before he finally said, "Nothing's going on. And I'm not accepting defeat."

"That's a relief," Taylor said, chuckling. "Let's go in and discuss this further over coffee."

Kyle held the ball in the crook of one arm, shaking his head as his brother led the way inside. Over the first cup of strong coffee, his hands began to thaw out. Taylor reminded him it hadn't been *his* idea to play basketball in December. Kyle would have liked nothing better than to wipe that smug smile off his youngest brother's face.

"Did Dad tell you that since Mitch and Raine and Joey won't be back from the Bahamas until next week, we won't be celebrating Christmas until the Sunday after?"

"Are you kidding? They've talked of little else. They're taking a *cruise* for Christmas. Our parents have never acted their age." Kyle scowled again.

"A couple of the guys at work are flying to Cancun for the holidays. Why don't you come with us?" Taylor asked.

"You're leaving, too?"

"Yeah. I just decided last night. With Raine and Mitch newlyweds and Mom and Dad acting like ones, I figured it wouldn't be a bad idea to try something new. You coming along?"

Kyle shook his head. "I'm doing the music at my boss's daughter's wedding on Christmas Eve."

For the first time in thirty-six years the Harrises wouldn't be together for Christmas. Kyle scowled, finished his third cup of coffee then switched to beer.

With his feet propped on Taylor's cluttered coffee table hours later, Kyle pretended to watch the game. But when the bell sounded at halftime, he had no idea who was ahead or which team had the ball. The announcer signed off for a station break and Kyle and Taylor both watched as a knight on a white horse galloped across the screen. Spear ready, the brave knight leapt across a moat and rescued a dark-haired maiden from the clutches of an evil king, all because the scent of her perfume lingered in his mind.

The maiden had dark eyes that contained a spark of emotion nearly as deep and indefinable as the one he'd seen in Clarissa's eyes. Kyle scowled again, and removed his feet from Taylor's coffee table.

"Ah, what I wouldn't do for a damsel in distress right about now," Taylor declared.

"Damsels in distress are hard to find these days," Kyle snapped, rising to his feet.

"Oh, they're out there, Kyle. They may not be wearing flowing white gowns, but they're out there. And I'll bet you Dad's old bowling trophy that I'll find one before you do."

"I told you to forget it, Tay. No more bets." Kyle stretched and gave his brother's apartment a distasteful leer. "This place looks like a dump."

"Changing the subject won't get you off the hook this time, Kyle. Besides, you've been itching for a fight all day and I'm not biting."

Without saying a word, Kyle carried his beer cans and coffee mug into the kitchen then shrugged into his coat. From the doorway, Taylor asked, "You sure nothing's wrong, Kyle?"

Kyle narrowed his eyes and thought about his brother's question. He was in a rotten mood, and wasn't even sure why. *What could possibly be wrong?* He shook his head, zipped up his coat and turned toward the door.

"We're not leaving for Cancun until the twenty-third. You should come along. Who knows how many damsels we'll meet down there. And these damsels won't be wearing long white gowns, Kyle. They'll be wearing bikinis. Tiny little bikinis."

The patch of rubber Kyle laid as he pulled away from the curb had been his only response to Taylor's statement. *Bikini-clad damsels, my eye.* He pressed his foot to the floor of his shiny red Mazda and sped down the highway toward his apartment.

Taylor was going to spend Christmas in Cancun, their parents were taking a cruise and Mitch, Raine and Joey were honeymooning in the Bahamas and wouldn't be back until the twenty-sixth. *Things were definitely changing.* It wasn't as if Kyle didn't like changes. He just liked to be the one in charge of them, that's all.

Taylor's ideas for a new bet were ridiculous. Damsels in distress had been replaced by nineties women. And nobody in his right mind would make a bet to be the first to have one kid, let alone three. Oh, no. He wasn't about to fall into any bet concerning kids. Little kids meant big responsibility. Little kids watched you without saying anything. And they asked questions, lots of questions. From a distance, they were fine. Some of his best friends used to be children. But little kids were just so—so damn little.

Mitch had taken to fatherhood like a fish to water. Even Taylor had taken an instant liking to Joey, Mitch's two-and-a-half-year-old son, a son he'd only learned he had a few months ago. But not Kyle. It wasn't that Joey wasn't a great kid—he had the Harris-blue eyes, and would, no doubt be a heartbreaker some day. But blue eyes or not, Joey made his Uncle Kyle edgy because Joey was a kid and kids made Kyle nervous. They had for a long, long time.

When a Christmas carol played over the car radio, he instantly pressed another button. Maybe he'd always been leery of kids, but he'd always liked Christmas. Oh, sure, he never did his shopping until the day before. But he waited until the last minute with practically everything he did.

There didn't seem to be any reason to do his shopping until *after* the twenty-fifth this year. As he sped down a long hill, another Christmas carol flowed through the speakers. This time Kyle didn't bother changing the station. It looked as if Christmas would come whether he spent it alone or not.

Clarissa parked close to the door, between the caterer's large van and a smaller one bearing the call letters of a local radio station. She closed her door then hurried to the back of the station wagon where a huge centerpiece was waiting to be carried inside.

The rain had turned to fat, wet snowflakes, only to melt the instant they touched the ground. Holiday enthusiasts were thrilled with the prospect of having a white Christmas this year. But Christmas was still a day away and knowing Philadelphia's weather, the snow could just as easily turn to rain.

Her boots splashed through a shallow puddle as she closed the station wagon's back door and hurried to the banquet room's protective awning. She managed to pull the door open and slip through without upsetting the floral arrangement. With precise care she placed the centerpiece on a decorated table and adjusted the guest book to a better angle.

"Hello, again."

Kyle's voice was low and smooth and she cursed its ability to make her pulse thud so rapidly. Taking a deep breath, she turned around slowly, tilting her chin up an inch at a time. "Hello, Kyle."

"We've got to stop meeting like this."

His voice had dipped lower, hinting at another meaning. She tried to square her shoulders against his allure, and for a full five seconds, it worked. But then he smiled, deepening a crease in one lean cheek. Her eyelids dropped, her shoulders lowered and whatever she'd been about to say slid right out of her mind.

A pan clanged against a pot in the kitchen, making Clarissa jump, and breaking the connection of their gazes. "I would have thought you'd have thought of something more original than that old come-on, Kyle."

"You want originality? I think I could come up with something." His voice was seductive, the inflection clear. His words held a challenge, but a touch of humor, too, and Clarissa smiled the tiniest bit in spite of herself.

She watched as his gaze slid down to her lips, and both their smiles drained away. She half expected him to say something provocative, something trite. She didn't expect him to cast her another half smile and saunter back to his stereo equipment.

Pulling her gaze from his retreating form wasn't easy. He had a swagger and a lazy sensuality that matched his voice. And judging from the self-confident set of his shoulders, she'd bet her bottom dollar he knew it.

Betting her bottom dollar wasn't in her plans. Neither was giving in to the kind of warmth a man like Kyle Harris could induce without even trying. She had a huge responsibility, what was proving to be a very successful business, and renewed hope. There was no place in her life, not even a tiny corner, for a man like Kyle Harris. Once was enough.

Within minutes the guests began to arrive and the reception was under way. She conferred with the caterers, congratulated the happy couple, confirmed a last-minute detail with the bride's mother and chatted with a few of the guests. She didn't catch the bouquet. And Kyle didn't ask her to dance. She told herself both were a tremendous relief.

Normally, she didn't stay for the wedding receptions she helped plan. She'd stayed for Raine and Mitch's because Raine was her assistant and one of her closest friends. However, from the onset of planning this wedding, things had gone wrong. Two major problems had cropped up, and several small ones. The caterers had canceled several weeks ago and another firm had to be found. The band, who had been friends of the young couple, had broken up, leaving them without music for the reception. It had been the bride's father who'd found someone to play the music, but Clarissa had vowed not to rest until she was certain everything had gone smoothly for her clients.

At five o'clock, the bride and groom left for their honeymoon. Shortly thereafter, the guests began to leave, too, and by six o'clock, Clarissa finally breathed a sigh of relief.

A short time later, she and Kyle were the only two people left in the building, and she could finally go home. She skimmed the instructions for the cleanup crew then flipped off all the lights except for one in Kyle's corner, where he was packing up his stereo equipment.

The opening chords of a Christmas ballad floated from the huge speakers near the dance floor. Placing the sheet of paper on the table, she turned toward the sound. Kyle was walking toward her, his strides long and slow, his gaze equally intent. He stopped a few feet away and, for an unhurried moment, studied her face, feature by feature.

"Alone at last," he finally whispered.

Her eyelids lowered slightly, but Clarissa found she couldn't look away. Not even when he tilted his head and reached for her hand.

Chapter Two

"Let's dance."

Kyle's voice lowered her eyelids farther, and his words lowered her resistance. Clarissa had felt his gaze on her all afternoon and had congratulated herself on her ability to keep a stiff upper lip and ignore him. Her lips didn't feel stiff at the moment. They felt soft and moist and the tiniest bit eager to open under his.

His hand was warm against hers, the pressure firm, and all male. If ever she'd been tempted to break a promise to herself, it was now. She took a deep breath, resisting the tug of his hand, and the tug of his smile. "It's getting late."

"It's early," he whispered in her ear.

Where was her resistance now? While Bing Crosby sang about Christmas dreams, Kyle settled his hand at her waist. Her right hand somehow found his shoulder, the other slid across his palm.

"He knew how to mellow out a Christmas song, didn't he?"

Kyle's voice, so close to her ear, came close to mellowing *her*. For a moment, the semidarkness, the holiday music, the broad hand at her waist and the breadth of shoulder beneath her fingertips seemed incredibly romantic, and she almost closed her eyes on a sigh. But a promise was a promise, and rather than allow herself to be pulled into his embrace, she let her hand trail down his arm, and turned away.

"What's wrong?" he said softly.

Without looking at him, she said, "Nothing's wrong. I just don't dance, that's all." She didn't cast him another glance, or offer him more of an explanation. She simply slipped through a nearby door and closed it behind her.

In the kitchen Clarissa closed her eyes on the last notes of "White Christmas." Why in the world had she told him she didn't dance? Physically, she could have. But she hadn't danced, not even once, in over five years.

She took her coat from a narrow cupboard and shrugged it over her shoulders. It reminded her how Kyle's hand had felt in exactly the same place. His palm had warmed her as he'd trailed it from her shoulder to her waist. It had been a long time since she'd felt warmed in that way. It had been a long time since she'd missed it. She shivered now, in spite of the warmth of her coat, and hurriedly rechecked the small kitchen, making certain everything was in its proper place when she already knew it was.

"You can come out now. I'm leaving."

The hint of seduction in his voice had been replaced with a touch of conceit. It grated on her nerves, but by the time she'd looked up from the boot she was pulling on, he'd disappeared.

He thinks I'm hiding from him! Of all the arrogant, self-centered, egotistical...

Clarissa told herself to calm down, and heard the outer door close. She told herself it didn't matter what he thought, and marched from the kitchen. She turned off the remaining light and locked the door behind her, still bristling.

Outside, the air had turned colder and a thin layer of snow clung to the branches of evergreen trees lining the parking lot. Large white flakes sifted down from the dark sky. With them, her irritation at Kyle drifted away. Excitement curled in her chest and reached outward. In that moment, nothing else mattered. It was Christmas Eve, and she was going home.

Everything was white, and more quiet than she could ever recall. It was as if the snow blanketing the entire city had absorbed all its sound, leaving them in a beautiful place where there were no footsteps, no traffic, only nature. Christmas Eve was awe-inspiring by itself, but the new-fallen snow somehow made it even more so.

Clarissa blinked a snowflake from her eyelashes and the words to "Winter Wonderland" floated through her mind. After unlocking her car door and inserting the key, she hummed a few verses. When the starter ground the first time, she stopped humming. When it ground the second time, she begged, "Please start. Please." On the third try, it made a horrible noise even the snow couldn't absorb, then ground away to nothingness.

The knock on her window kept her from trying a fourth time. Kyle Harris pointed toward the front of her car and said, "If you're through hiding, release the latch for the hood."

For one tiny moment, she felt her jaw slacken in surprise. Irritation immediately followed. She clamped her mouth shut and pulled the knob to release the hood at the same time. Striving for calm, she pushed open her door and strode to the front of the car where Kyle was fidgeting with something or other.

"I was not hiding!"

"Sure you were." He didn't bother to look up from the engine when he added, "Try it again."

Clarissa didn't move. She wasn't sure what it was he expected her to try again. She hadn't been hiding from him, no matter what he thought. She could stand around arguing the point, but she had a feeling he'd never believe her. *Damn.*

"Such an undignified remark from a refined lady. I like that in a woman."

She hadn't realized she'd cursed out loud, and wondered if he realized what he did to her. He exasperated her, and mollified her at the same time. His voice was calm, his gaze steady. Both held a trace of laughter, and a thread of longing that settled over her as gently as the snowflakes falling from the dark sky.

"Do you have any idea what's wrong with my car?"

When his voice came, it was so deep, so low, she doubted he was thinking about cars. "Taylor's the mechanic in the family. Although I dated a female mechanic for a while, I'm afraid her engine expertise didn't rub off."

Clarissa wished he hadn't said *rub.* It conjured up too many images, warm images, images she wouldn't let herself dwell on.

Kyle hadn't expected Clarissa to let him get away with that crack about undignified remarks from refined ladies, or about his lack of engine expertise. But then, he hadn't expected her to look at him the way she was looking at him right now, either. The cold air had reddened her cheeks, but the brown eyes gazing into his were far from cold. He moved closer, thinking a man could wander into the warmth of her eyes and get lost for days on end.

Kyle stood in the hushed stillness of the night, thinking that getting lost with Clarissa Cohagan was incredibly intriguing. He felt the cold imprint of a snowflake that had landed on his cheek, and watched her gaze follow its trail as it melted and ran down his neck, wishing her mouth would do the same.

"Looks like you're going to have to leave your car here overnight," he whispered.

"Yes," she whispered in return.

"I'll give you a ride home."

She glanced around the parking lot before answering. "I live in Quakertown, and I couldn't impose. But I'd appreciate it if you'd give me a lift to the nearest gas station."

He saw her shiver, and held the van door open for her before hurrying around to the driver's side. As a blast of cool air seeped through his coat, he remembered his brother's latest bet. Taylor had told him there were damsels in distress out here. This particular damsel was stranded on Christmas Eve. Problem was, she didn't want rescuing. He'd like to give her a lift, all right. Straight to his place. There was only one thing keeping him from suggesting it.

He removed his glove with his teeth and dug into his pocket for his keys. He started the engine then nonchalantly asked, "Will your husband come for you?"

"It's a long drive from Timbuktu."

"Timbuktu?"

The light from the dash didn't reach his face, yet Clarissa could imagine exactly how he looked. One strong hand gripped the steering wheel, the other lay comfortably along the armrest. His head was tilted to one side, gazing at her in the dark, and she imagined his eyes, as blue as the first Christmas morning, were studying her with a curious intensity.

"As far as I know, that's where Jonathan, my *ex*-husband, is."

She caught a movement along his profile. Although it was too dark to tell for sure, she had a feeling he was smiling. He swerved through the deserted parking lot then back out again.

"Where are you going?"

"To Quakertown. I'm taking you home."

"Listen, Kyle, I make it a rule to be totally indepen-
dent."

He changed lanes and turned the windshield wipers a
notch faster. "Clarissa...what do people call you? Clare?
Riss? Rissie?"

Her indignation lowered her voice. "If they want me to
answer, they call me Clarissa."

"Clarissa, huh? I'll have to work on that. Well, Clarissa,
rules were made to be broken. Besides, 'tis the season."

He flicked on the radio and a rather unique rendition of
"Jingle Bells," performed by barking dogs, filled the van's
interior. With the silly song, her indignation evaporated. It
was Christmas Eve and even at twenty-nine years old, she
felt the excitement of this night, its special magic.

When that song ended, soft strains of "Silent Night" took
its place. Kyle sang along, his voice vibrating through the
softly sung lyrics. "I wonder what Christmas will be like in
the Bahamas or in Cancun or aboard a cruise ship."

"Are you going away for the holidays?"

"No. My family is."

"You mean you'll be alone on Christmas?" Clarissa
thought about her Christmas, the decorated tree, the gifts
hidden in the attic. And the special person waiting to share
it all with her.

"Just me and my shadow," he said dryly.

She tried not to hear the silver-edged echo in his resonant
voice. She tried to ignore the angelic voices of a children's
choir singing another carol over the radio. She tried to tell
herself Kyle Harris couldn't possibly be lonely. But Clarissa understood too much about loneliness to misinterpret
its tinny echoes in another person's voice.

"You could come to my house tomorrow," she said.

For a moment, a street lamp threw a long beam of light
over Kyle's face. She wasn't sure who was more surprised by
her invitation, her or Kyle, and suddenly wanted to call back

her words. "Here's my street," she said, instead. "My place is in the middle of the next block."

He pulled the van up in front of her house and turned to face her. "You're inviting me to spend Christmas with you?"

His voice had taken on that sultry-nights-and-rumpled-sheets tone. She wished she could think of some way to let him know she wasn't interested in rumpling sheets. Not with Kyle. Not with anyone.

"Does that mean you're coming?" she asked.

"I'd love to."

Suddenly, she couldn't put two thoughts together. It was that voice of his. It did crazy things to a woman, made her feel soft and warm, in spite of the winter temperatures. The man was too attractive for his own good. But he probably already knew that. He was too intriguing, as well, and Clarissa imagined he knew that, too. She looked away from him, trying to think of some way to thank him for the ride, and let him know there could never be anything between them.

From the corner of her eye she saw the curtain at her front window flutter. There it was—the way to show him she couldn't get involved with him, or anyone else. She wouldn't have to say a thing. Tomorrow morning, he'd see for himself.

"Thanks for the ride home."

"Thank you for inviting me."

"You're welcome," she answered. "Besides, my little girl will love having company on Christmas."

"Your little girl?"

"Yes. She's five years old and her name's Stephanie. See you about eleven."

The door clicked shut before Kyle could say goodbye, but then he wasn't sure he'd have been able to say anything, anyway. *Her little girl?*

He was going to spend Christmas with Clarissa and *her five-year-old daughter?* Why hadn't she told him that she had a kid?

Maybe because he hadn't asked.

What was he going to say to a little girl on Christmas? Too bad he couldn't call Taylor and Mitch. They'd know what to do. Mitch had always *liked* little kids. Even Taylor seemed *comfortable* around them.

At a red light, Kyle's thoughts idled along with the van's engine. He wondered what Mitch was doing in the Bahamas and Taylor in Cancun, beneath a hot sun on stretches of white sand. When the light turned green, he took his foot from the brake. What were they doing? Mitch was on his honeymoon and Taylor had gone to one of the hottest singles' spots in the world. It didn't take a genius or a great imagination to figure out what they were probably doing at this very moment.

He, on the other hand, was here, in southeastern Pennsylvania, where it was wet and cold, on his own with a woman who rarely smiled, whose brown eyes hinted at things he couldn't even imagine. He'd be spending his Christmas with a *little* kid, when he knew darn well that little kids made him nervous as hell.

Over the radio, another little kid, one who couldn't have carried a tune in a basket, was singing "I Saw Mommy Kissing Santa Claus." Kyle momentarily forgot about kids in general and thought about kissing Clarissa in particular. He'd been intrigued by the pout on her lips from the moment he'd met her. He wouldn't mind kissing that pouting mouth. He wouldn't mind in the least.

Mitch and Taylor could have their sun and sand this Christmas. Kyle wouldn't have traded places with them for the world.

"How long before he's here, Mommy?"

Clarissa encircled Stephanie's slender wrist, the one

adorned with a new watch, and bent her head near her daughter's. "When the big hand is on the twelve and the little hand is on the eleven."

"At twelve-eleven?" Big brown eyes, full of question, looked up into hers.

"No, honey, at eleven o'clock." With a mother-soft voice, Clarissa explained about *o'clock* and *thirty* and counting by fives.

"When do you suppose it will be eleven o'clock?" Stephanie said.

"In thirty-five minutes."

"Oh. A long time," the little girl said.

That depended on whether one was a child or an adult. To Stephanie, thirty-five minutes seemed like forever. To Clarissa, who looked around her at the clutter of torn wrapping paper, crinkled tissue paper, curling ribbons and discarded boxes, thirty-five minutes wasn't long at all.

"Do you suppose Mr. Abernathy will be able to stay awake long enough to see my new tape recorder?" Stephanie asked.

Mr. Abernathy had moved into the back apartment the day before Halloween. Shortly thereafter, Stephanie had begun to request tea with her meals. Also about that time, *do you suppose* became the first three words of ninety percent of her questions.

Clarissa smiled then pressed her lips to her daughter's smooth forehead. "I suppose Mr. Abernathy would like that very much."

"Goody! Don't you just love Christmas, Mommy?"

She *just loved* her daughter. "Yes, I do, sweetheart."

Stephanie struggled to stand, her leg brace bumping against the coffee table. Clarissa automatically reached to help her little girl up. Unblinking brown eyes, almost identical in color to her own, stared up at her. Like a looking glass into her heart, Stephanie's feelings were mirrored there in her eyes. Trust, love, happiness, and today, excitement.

Sprinkled around the edges was a touch of stubbornness which could sometimes be almost invisible or seem a mile wide.

The child pushed herself to her feet and, with the use of crutches, hurried to the door, a new red tape recorder dangling from the strap around her shoulders. At the door, she looked up at her mother. "How many minutes now?"

"Thirty-four." Clarissa softened her answer with a smile.

"Still a long time," Stephanie said before hurrying through the doorway.

Grabbing a cellophane-wrapped fruit basket, Clarissa followed the rhythmic *thunk, thud, thunk, thud* of Stephanie's shoes and crutches as she sped with amazing velocity down the long hallway toward the back of the house. The door was opened, and she heard Stephanie say, "Merry Christmas, Mr. Abernathy."

"And to you, child. Come in, come in. Oh, Mrs. Cohagan," he added when she reached his door. "It's good to see you, too. I've just brewed a pot of tea."

Clarissa smiled as she handed the old gentleman the fruit basket. Stephanie adored their neighbor, was in fact convinced he was Santa Claus himself. Stephanie had had enough pain and suffering in her life, and Clarissa didn't have the heart to tell her the truth. Besides, she couldn't blame her daughter. If there really was a Santa Claus, Mr. Abernathy would definitely fit the description, from his white hair, to his red suspenders, all the way down to his thick wool socks.

The old man led the way through the narrow living room with surprising agility for a man his age, Clarissa and Stephanie following close behind. Walking straight to the table, he took the squat teapot in hand and raised one bushy eyebrow in Clarissa's direction, silently asking her to join him for a cup of tea.

"I'd love to stay, Mr. Abernathy, but I can't today. I just wanted to say Merry Christmas and tell you how much I appreciate the times you watch Stephanie for me."

"The pleasure, it is all mine," he declared, pushing a huge plate of cookies her way. "You don't have time for even one small cookie?"

The plate contained nearly every kind of cookie imaginable, and it was Clarissa's turn to raise her eyebrows. "Where in the world did you get so many cookies?" she asked.

Stephanie giggled and took a seat. "From all the children who leave cookies for him on Christmas Eve, Mommy."

Clarissa knew Stephanie honestly believed their sprightly neighbor was Santa Claus. Christmas morning was hardly the time to tell her differently.

Mr. Abernathy winked at Clarissa and said, "I received these cookies from friends."

"You must have a lot of friends," she said, laughing.

"Surely a fine woman like yourself has many friends, too."

Before Clarissa could answer, Stephanie said, "Mostly Mommy's friends are doctors and nurses. Right, Mommy?"

Running her hand along her daughter's fine hair, Clarissa smiled. "And Raine. She's our friend."

"Yeah," Stephanie agreed. "And don't forget the new friend you invited to spend Christmas with us."

Kyle Harris, her friend? Clarissa wasn't about to get into a discussion about that. Besides, after today, she doubted she'd ever see him again.

"Stephanie was afraid you'd be asleep," Clarissa said. "If you're too busy..."

"My busiest season has just come to an end. I was about to have a cookie before I settle down for a nice winter's nap. Stephanie, you will join me for tea, yes?"

The child nodded, and the old gentleman added, "Do not worry, Mrs. Cohagan, I will send her home when our tea is gone."

Stephanie called goodbye to her mother and, waiting until she heard the door click shut, smiled across the table at her sprightly neighbor. With wonder and innocence she wasn't even aware she had, she watched as Mr. Abernathy yawned. He patted his stomach and offered her the plate of cookies. She chose the largest gingerbread man she could find and promptly bit off his head then took a loud sip of her milky tea.

"Tell me, child, did you get everything you wanted for Christmas?"

Stephanie, who was thoughtful as she chewed her cookie, didn't answer until she'd emptied her mouth and had taken another sip of her tea. "Mommy got me this tape recorder and a new dolly. Grandma sent a new dress from Florida and *you* know what else was under the tree. But there was no daddy, Mr. Abernathy. Amy Jo Parker got a new baby brother yesterday, just like she wanted. Do you suppose I'll have to wait until next year and ask for a daddy again?"

For a moment, Stephanie was mesmerized by the twinkle in Mr. Abernathy's sparkling blue eyes. "Not all Christmas wishes arrive at Christmastime, you know."

"They don't?" she asked.

Laying a finger at the side of his nose, he gently toyed with his snow-white mustache. "No, child," he answered thoughtfully. "Christmas is a magical time, one that doesn't always conform to the time frames of mere mortals. Christmas wishes are special indeed, and can arrive anytime. Sometimes they come on Christmas morning, sometimes weeks later. Why, I remember one little boy who, many years ago, received his Christmas wish on the Fourth of July."

"I didn't know that!" With renewed hope, she tipped up her teacup, emptied the last drop and replaced it in its saucer. "Do you mean I could ask for a daddy, and a new baby brother like Amy Jo Parker?"

Mr. Abernathy's chuckle started slow, and deepened, until his shoulders moved and his round belly shook beneath his flannel shirt. "I think it would be best for your mother if you asked for one wish at a time, don't you?"

Stephanie nodded then turned serious. "Mommy doesn't believe you're real."

"I'm afraid your mother has lost a bit of her belief in Christmas magic, but I have a feeling she'll be getting it back again. Now tell me, child. This friend who's coming today. He is a man, yes?"

Stephanie's eyes opened wide and her mouth rounded into an O. "Yes." She giggled. "Oh, Mr. Abernathy, yes."

Clarissa left the door ajar for Stephanie and hurried around the apartment. She'd basted the turkey breast and poked the squash. She'd arranged the tiny petits fours Stephanie had requested for dessert on a fancy plate then set about picking up the wrapping paper from beneath the Christmas tree. The thud from the hall didn't draw her gaze. Accustomed to her daughter's noises, she waited for the sound of crutches hitting wood.

"Merry Christmas."

She didn't remember straightening or turning around, but realized she must have because she was suddenly looking across the narrow room, straight into Kyle's eyes.

"You're early."

"I know." He didn't sound the least bit contrite, and again Clarissa thought he was too attractive for his own good, from his windblown honey-blond hair all the way down to his worn brown loafers. "Can I come in?" he asked, already shouldering his way through the doorway.

She hurried to open the door farther, wondering how he expected a woman to think straight when he was looking at her like that. In his arms he carried several brightly wrapped packages. The top one teetered, and even though he tried to keep it from falling, it began a fast slide down the stack. Clarissa caught it just before it would have hit the floor.

The gift was practically weightless, yet it shook in her hands, because the tag said *Rissa*. She straightened, taking in the scent of leather and cold winter air that clung to Kyle, taking in the slight cleft in his chin she hadn't noticed before, and the way his smile creased one cheek.

"No one calls me Rissa."

"Someone does now."

"You brought gifts." Clarissa wasn't sure what she'd expected, but she hadn't expected a gift, or the nickname penned in his masculine scrawl.

"It's Christmas." He seemed to think those two words explained everything, his reason for bringing gifts, and his reason for shortening her name.

"But I don't have anything for you."

His gaze dropped to her mouth, and slowly lowered farther. Her eyelids grew heavy, and she felt a pull, almost magical, drawing them closer. His look sparked an ache in her chest, an ache for her lost belief in men and their staying power. She felt a moment's remorse for her loss, for there had been a time when she'd believed in magic and in passion and love. But time and circumstances had taken a toll on her belief in those things.

"You think you don't have anything for me? That's where you're wrong, Rissa."

That, she should have expected. She tried not to bristle, but it wasn't easy. Men like Kyle Harris seemed to think with a certain part of their anatomy far below their brains.

Taking another package from the top of the stack, she asked, "When did you have time to shop?"

"Last night." His gaze came back to hers, and silence loomed between them. Her nerves were out of tempo with the Christmas music coming from the kitchen and she suddenly wondered how she was going to get through the afternoon.

"Where's your daughter?" he asked, glancing around the room.

Clarissa took a deep breath and stepped around him, placing the gifts beneath the tree. "She's visiting a friend in the back apartment. She'll be here in a few minutes."

Kyle placed the remaining gifts under the tree, wondering at the sudden change in Rissa. When he'd first arrived, the look in her eyes had had his heart thumping like bongo drums keeping time to Colombian music. In a matter of a few moments, she'd cooled toward him. He wondered why.

"You went Christmas shopping on Christmas Eve?" she asked conversationally.

He shrugged out of his coat and handed it to her. "Nothing like a little intense last-minute shopping on Christmas Eve to get you in the mood."

He knew she'd heard the double entendre. He saw it in her eyes, but she wasn't responding to him. She wasn't laughing, either, or putting him in his place with some scathing remark. What was going on?

Rhythmic thuds drew his gaze. He felt his eyes open in surprise as a little girl sped into the room on crutches. She whipped past her mother with an agility that surprised him, and stopped, her gaze climbing up him like a mountain climber eyeing a new ridge.

"Hi," she said, grinning. "My name's Stephanie, and I think you'll do just fine. Can I call you daddy?"

Kyle, who somehow managed to keep his mouth from dropping open, glanced from the child, who was looking at him as if he were some high-tech toy she wanted to play with before reading the directions first, to her mother, who wore the same dumbfounded expression he did.

This was exactly why little kids made Kyle nervous. They were totally unpredictable, asking questions and making statements adults were hard put to answer.

Clarissa went down to her knees and took the little girl's chin in her hand. "Stephanie, honey, of course you *can't* call him daddy. This is Mr. Harris."

"You mean I didn't get him for Christmas?" the child asked in a small voice.

Kyle watched as Clarissa shook her head firmly, her gaze seeking his. There was no question she was as surprised by her daughter's question as he was. Something else suddenly became clear. Clarissa's gaze had been as warm and smooth as velvet when she'd first laid eyes on him across the room. Mention of her daughter had turned her look to cool, brown satin, and he was beginning to understand why. She hadn't expected Stephanie's question. But she had expected him to take one look at those crutches and leg braces and hightail it out of there.

Without waiting for an invitation, he sank into a chair and stretched his legs out in front of him. The little girl smiled at him, and he felt something go soft in the pit of his stomach. Next thing Kyle knew, he was smiling back.

"Mr. Harris?"

"Mr. Harris is my father's name. Everyone I know calls me Kyle."

Stephanie giggled, as if she understood. "Kyle, do you suppose I could open my presents now?"

Kyle eyed the gifts he'd brought and that Clarissa had placed under the tree, his mouth suddenly going dry. The gifts he'd bought. The kid wanted to open her gifts.

He stammered, trying to think of some excuse. But in the end, all he could do was nod.

Chapter Three

Before Clarissa's eyes, Kyle's expression changed. She usually prided herself on her ability to read people's body language. It was a tremendous help in dealing with nervous brides and grooms, worried mothers and doting fathers. But Kyle's body language was sending her a mixed message. She'd fully expected him to clear his throat and suddenly remember he had someplace he *had* to be, to take one look at Stephanie's handicap and leave. The men in Clarissa's life had a tendency to do that.

Stephanie was chatting, and although Kyle nodded, he didn't appear to be following the conversation. He seemed unsure what to do next, but one thing was certain. He wasn't preparing to leave.

The sound of crinkling paper drew her gaze to her daughter, who had plopped to the floor next to the tree, smoothing her red velour dress over her brace-clad legs straight in front of her. Stephanie's eyes sparkled and, grasping the gift in both hands, she giggled with joy. Taking a deep breath, Clarissa offered a silent prayer of thanks for her daughter's happiness, and felt that happiness steal into her own heart.

Kyle silently cursed his choice of gifts. Looking at the little girl with her huge brown eyes and enough plastic and metal on her legs to build a radio tower, he mentally prepared himself for the tears and disappointment he'd undoubtedly see in the girl's eyes. He knew he was no good with kids, and he didn't relish the thought of ruining this one's Christmas. But dammit, he hadn't known.

Stephanie screeched with pleasure as she tore into the colorful paper, but it was Clarissa's answering laughter that filtered through his worry. Her laugh was deep and throaty, and looking at her, he felt as if he was glimpsing something few people saw—Clarissa Cohagan, relaxed and happy.

She sat on the floor near her daughter. Wisps of hair had escaped the barrette at her nape, tangling with the wreath earrings dangling from her ears. She leaned back on one arm, her position practically inviting him to check out curves her clothing had only hinted at. Her dark blue sweater reached from her neck to her thighs, draping softly over the swell of her breasts and the curve of her hips. Her legs were drawn up, one knee crossed over the other, and were covered with a stretchy material the same color as her sweater.

Still laughing, her gaze met his. The look in her eyes dragged at him, and he felt his desire for her making its presence known. He shifted in his seat and crossed his legs.

"Winter Wonderland" strummed from a portable radio in another room, and he had a sudden image of another kind of wonderland, one in which he took Clarissa's hand in his and led her to the center of the floor. He'd press her body close, close enough to feel her breasts against his chest, close enough to feel her breath on his neck as they slowly swayed to lovers' music.

Stephanie's second bout of screeches drew both their gazes. There were no tears on her small face. Only a look of wide-eyed wonder as she lifted her new roller skates from the box. Relief coursed through Kyle. He grinned at the little girl, but when he looked at Clarissa, the sheen of tears in *her* eyes drained his smile away.

He prided himself on being somewhat of a ladies' man. Somewhat, hell. He felt downright lofty about his ability to ignite his lover's desire, to expertly take her to extreme heights of passion. But he didn't have a clue to the reason for the haunted look in this woman's eyes.

"Roller skates!" Stephanie exclaimed, already reaching to slide them over her shoes.

"Stephanie." Clarissa's hand stilled her daughter's movements. "Kyle didn't know about your braces. You can't keep these skates."

"But he gave them to me."

"I know, sweetheart. But you can't keep them."

Kyle had seen Joey, his nephew, gearing up for a temper tantrum often enough to recognize the gathering storm in Stephanie's eyes. Mitch probably would have known what to do to ward it off. Kyle hadn't a clue.

"But why?"

That was it. No temper tantrum, no tears. Just two little words and eyes that held so much open longing and hope, Kyle, for one, would have been more comfortable with the tantrum. He'd never heard a tinier voice, or sensed so much need in one little kid's expression.

The fringe of Stephanie's lashes cast a shadow on her cheeks as she looked up at him. It was that shadow more than anything that caused Kyle's stomach to knot, and his chest to expand, that made him feel like a knight on a white horse about to rescue a tiny damsel in distress. It was that vulnerable shadow that made him say, "She won't hurt anything by trying them on."

Stephanie beamed. Clarissa didn't. There was a long, brittle silence before she handed her daughter another package to unwrap, and cast him a sharp glance. "Why don't you open this one, honey, while I show Kyle the place mat you made for me in school.''

The warm tone of voice she used for her daughter was a contradiction to the cool glare she directed at him. That look told him that Stephanie wasn't *his* responsibility. It also reminded him that he'd overstepped his boundaries. But if Clarissa thought her stern-faced expression would get to him, she had another think coming. He'd grown up with two brothers close on his heels and had learned at an early age how to cajole his way out of sticky situations.

She was angry. Anger, he could deal with, much better in fact than the look of quiet, soul-rending need he'd seen in the kid's eyes, or the helplessness he'd felt when he thought she was about to burst into tears.

He watched as Clarissa found her feet, as lithe and agile as a dancer. He liked the way her hair waved down her back, the way her sweater pulled tight in the front, and found himself looking forward to this next confrontation. He moved his ankle off his knee and stood, slowly following Clarissa from the room. Watching the smooth sway of her hips, he found that there were several things he looked forward to trying with this woman.

The door had no sooner swished shut behind them than she turned on him, hands on hips. ''You'll have to take those skates back.''

''She loves them.''

''Kyle. She uses crutches and has braces on her legs.''

''I noticed.''

''Those braces don't come off at whim, you know. She can't roller-skate.''

''She wasn't going to skate. She just wants to try them on.'' Kyle didn't pretend to know a whole lot about little kids. But he did know that the one out in the living room liked the roller skates he'd given her for Christmas. He didn't understand why Clarissa was so upset about that.

"What happened to her?" he asked. "Why does she have to wear those braces?"

Even with the deep breath Clarissa took, Kyle saw her bottom lip quiver with the effort to make him understand. Lowering her voice to barely more than a whisper, she said, "Stephanie was born with a birth defect."

Her voice cracked, and he wondered at the look deep in her eyes. He didn't wonder what it meant. He recognized guilt when he saw it.

"The doctors told me she'd never walk in braces, let alone without them," she stated. "They were wrong. I've seen her through three operations and weekly physical therapy for the past five years. One more operation, a major one, and the doctors say she *may* be able to walk without braces. I can't risk a broken bone. Not when we've come so far."

Again, Kyle saw the sheen of tears illuminate her eyes. Again, he saw her blink them away. He would have liked to push the hair from her forehead, to press his palm to her face. To offer her comfort. But she didn't look ready to accept his comfort. In fact, she looked as if she might shatter into a thousand pieces if he so much as touched her.

He lowered his voice, but couldn't help the huskiness that nearly suffocated his next words. "What do you want me to do?"

Her face had paled, and something soul-deep glittered in her eyes. She pressed her lips together and turned from him. "I want you to enjoy your day with us. And when you leave, I want you to take those skates with you."

He understood what she said. And what she didn't say. She hadn't expected him to stay this long. And after today, she didn't expect him to come back. The realization straightened his spine, because as he looked at the slender column of her neck and remembered the way her eyes could change from warm to cool without any warning, Kyle knew he wanted to come back. He wanted to touch his lips to the smooth skin at her temple, to watch her eyelids lower as he flicked his tongue across the bow of her lower lip.

"All right," he said.

"What do you mean *all right?*"

She'd turned her head to look at him. Her eyes had narrowed, as if she was suspicious of his motives. He managed to keep a smile off his face, because she had every reason to be suspicious. And because he had every intention of getting to know her better. A lot better.

He'd known there was something between them the first time he'd laid eyes on her at Mitch's wedding. He'd glimpsed an answering awareness in her eyes a time or two. The fact that she didn't give in to it didn't detract from its power, but it did sharpen his senses and make him more determined than ever to see her again. Truth was, he was attracted to Clarissa Cohagan. And whether she admitted it or not, the feeling was mutual.

Two things Kyle knew about were hit singles, and women. He could sing the lyrics and hum the melody of every song recorded over the past twenty years. And he'd known enough women in his thirty-six years to make an average guy more than a little smug.

It was pretty obvious this woman didn't wholly trust him, but Kyle figured she probably had a good reason for that. So, he wouldn't rush her. He'd lead her into a dance so slow she wouldn't realize he was the one doing the leading.

"What do you mean *all right?*" she repeated.

It took a moment for her question to register, and when it did, it was all he could do not to strut. "I mean all right. You have my word. When I leave here this afternoon, I'll take those skates with me."

"Then you understand?"

He eyed her thoughtfully before answering. "Yes. And no. But it doesn't matter. You have my word."

"Good."

With that, they both turned toward the door and joined Stephanie, who was still sitting near the Christmas tree where she was trying to fit her shoe into one of the roller skates. "Stephanie, honey," Clarissa said. "Let's see what other gifts you have to open. Kyle didn't know about your braces. He's going to have to take those skates back to the store."

Stephanie's head jerked toward Kyle. He winked at her as he made a show of dribbling a round package wrapped in snowman paper. "Don't worry, Stef," he promised. "Your mom explained about your braces, and since we don't want you to break any bones, I'll just keep the skates for you at my place."

Kyle Harris, you are good. He'd come up with a way to prevent the kid from being disappointed, and continue to see her mother at the same time. Yessiree, two things he knew about were definitely songs, and women.

"You mean I can still use them sometimes?" Stephanie asked in a small voice.

She wanted to use them sometimes? He hadn't thought of that. "I guess so." He looked from Stephanie to Clarissa, and felt some of his smugness dissolve.

"Can you guarantee you'll catch her if she falls?" Clarissa asked.

Kyle paled, suddenly feeling inadequate. Clarissa wanted a guarantee that he'd keep her daughter safe? He was just a carefree bachelor. What did he know about keeping little kids safe?

Clarissa saw the panic in Kyle's eyes, suddenly understanding what it was about him that made her leery. He reminded her of Jonathan, Stephanie's father. It wasn't that they looked alike. Jonathan was dark, Kyle wasn't. But they both had a sensuality that could cause thermal-curtain meltdown in three seconds or less. They walked with similar swaggers, had the same glint in their eyes that said *male on the prowl.*

More than anything else, though, it was the way Kyle was staring at Stephanie's leg braces, and the way he'd panicked when she'd asked if he could guarantee he'd keep Stephanie from hurting herself in those roller skates. Her little girl's handicap made Kyle as jumpy as a cat on hot bricks. Jonathan hadn't been able to handle the responsibility, either. That was why he'd left.

Clarissa had been bitter about Jonathan's desertion for a long time. But she wasn't bitter anymore. Besides, Stephanie's handicap wasn't Kyle's responsibility. He'd gone out of his way to buy those presents. It wasn't his fault he'd bought her something she couldn't use. He hadn't known.

Watching him dribble a silly round package he'd brought had her smiling almost as much as Stephanie. The man was a charmer, there was no doubt about it. And he'd made her daughter's Christmas special, in spite of his choice of gifts. Clarissa felt her heart soften at the look in Stephanie's eyes. She softened even more when she looked into Kyle's.

She didn't doubt, not for one minute, that this would be the last time she saw him. But he was here for now. And it was Christmas, after all.

"Do you suppose that's a basketball, Mommy?"

"Could be," she replied.

"Does Kyle have to keep that at his house, too?"

It was Kyle who answered. "I don't think that'll be necessary, Stef. There are lots of ways you can play basketball that are safe. Just don't ever try it with my brother Tay. He stepped on my foot so hard the last time we played I limped most of this week. And just look at what he did to my hands."

Honestly, Clarissa thought. Wasn't it just like a man to expound upon his injuries?

"Wow," Stephanie exclaimed. "Look, Mommy!"

Kyle held his hands out for her to see, and she couldn't bring herself to tell him she'd had hangnails more serious than his little scrape. His hands were thick, his fingers long, and from somewhere, she remembered a saying comparing the size of a man's hands to the size of his . . .

"You should ask Mommy to kiss it and make it all better."

Stephanie's statement produced a potent image in Clarissa's mind. She continued to stare at his hands, and imagined them on her body, imagined them in places she hadn't dreamed of being touched in years. Her gaze finally climbed to his eyes, and she felt her cheeks grow warm. Kyle shifted in his chair, as if his imagination was conjuring up similar fantasies.

"Do you want her to?" Stephanie asked.

He settled himself deeper into the cushion on the chair, and brought one ankle up to his other knee. "Thanks for the offer, Stef. Maybe another time."

It suddenly seemed too warm in the room. Clarissa kept her gaze trained on her daughter, but it was several seconds before her eyes actually focused on her child.

"Why do you call me Stef?" the little girl asked.

Kyle cocked his head to one side and said, "Even though Stephanie is a beautiful name, it's pretty long. You call a person by a nickname and you get to their real personality. I cut everyone's name down to one syllable."

"What's a syllable?"

Oh-oh. Kyle, who had gotten into *why* trouble with Joey a time or two, tried to come up with a simple answer to the kid's question. "A syllable is like one note in a song, or one beat of a drum. Stef is one syllable." He tapped his thigh one time. Tapping it three times, he said, "Steph-a-nie has three."

Stephanie giggled as she asked, "How many syllables in Mr. Abernathy?"

Kyle tapped his thigh six times. "Six."

"I don't think Mr. Abernathy would like it if I called him Ab, do you, Mommy?" Without waiting for her mother's reply, the child began to tear into the wrapping paper covering the round package, proclaiming she'd always wanted a real basketball.

In record time Stephanie had opened her two other gifts, a puzzle and a soft toy cat, its fur so long and plush and white, she immediately named it Abbie, because she said it reminded her of Mr. Abernathy's soft white beard. At the mention of her neighbor, she eyed Kyle thoughtfully. "Do you believe in Santa, Kyle?"

Clarissa expected him to stammer out an answer, and was just about to come to his rescue by changing the subject when he said, "Doesn't everybody?"

"I knew it!" Stephanie declared. "Mr. Abernathy told me my daddy would believe in Christmas magic." Before either Kyle or Clarissa could say a word, she added, "Mommy, do you suppose we could eat? I'm starving."

It was second nature to help Stephanie to her feet. It was second nature to push her daughter's hair from her face then watch as she lithely maneuvered herself around the furniture and headed for the kitchen. And it was second nature to feel pride swell in her chest at her little girl's determination and unfailing spirit.

"I don't know how you keep up with her," Kyle said softly.

She smiled at him and replied, "She can be a handful."

Clarissa had said that statement so many times it, too, had become second nature. But she'd never said it to a man whose gaze had lazily roamed the front of her sweater, making *handful* take on an entirely different meaning.

He leaned forward in his chair, and if she lived to be a hundred and ten, she doubted she'd forget the lofty glint in his eyes. She placed her hands on her hips with the intention of putting an end to the awareness arcing between them, but her stance made her all the more aware of the way her sweater followed the contours of her body.

"You, Kyle Harris, have a dirty mind."

He stood, and she was finally able to tear her gaze away from his. Halfway to the kitchen, she heard him say, "If you know what I'm thinking, I'm not the only one."

In the kitchen Stephanie was already busily traipsing from counter to table, carefully placing spoons and forks next to their plates. Keeping up a steady prattle to Kyle, she had no idea everyone didn't place utensils and napkins in baskets with sturdy handles, perfect for grasping while maneuvering crutches.

Clarissa was glad Kyle's attention was diverted. It kept him occupied elsewhere, which gave her time to get her wayward thoughts under control. It had been a long time since she'd been as aware of her own body as she had been beneath Kyle's gaze a few minutes ago.

While she sliced the turkey, she reminded herself of Kyle's similarities to Jonathan. But when she placed the platter into Kyle's waiting hands, she completely forgot what it was she'd been telling herself. All she could think about was the way those hands of his would feel on her.

Determined not to give him any more encouragement, she placed the remaining dishes on the table and took a seat. To his credit, Kyle behaved like a perfect gentleman throughout the meal, regaling them with stories of his childhood that were anything but gentlemanly.

When they'd finished their meal, Stephanie asked him to help her put her new puzzle together, and Clarissa found herself alone in the kitchen. She could have left the dishes, but she wanted something to do to keep herself busy, something to keep her from watching the interaction between Kyle and her child.

While systematically washing the dishes, she listened to the chatter in the next room. Stephanie sounded so happy, laughing and playing. Clarissa hated to see it end, but knew it would. There was nothing she wouldn't do for her daughter. She'd move mountains, build bridges, take her to the clouds if it would make her happy. Tomorrow, she'd have to explain about daddies, and counting only on one-self. Tomorrow, but not today.

Deep in thought, she hadn't noticed the silence until she'd finished drying the last dish. Folding the towel, she turned to investigate. Her movements froze. Her eyes widened.

Kyle stood just inside the doorway, leaning against the counter. Watching her.

"How long have you been standing there?"

"Not long."

"Where's Stephanie?"

He took a step toward her before answering. "She fell asleep on the couch a few minutes ago." There was a mo-ment's silence before he asked, "What were you thinking about? Just now, I mean."

His look told her he *knew* what she'd been thinking about earlier, when she'd found him staring at her with a kind of blatant longing that only a man could manage. With her thoughts, her gaze automatically traveled down to his hands, and for the first time, she noticed he held a package in each.

"You didn't have to bring gifts today."

"I wanted to." Moving closer, his voice dropped in vol-ume. "There are a lot of things I want to do with you, Rissa."

"*Clar*issa," she corrected. Reaching for the larger pack-age, she said, "I thought you said you shortened every-body's name to one syllable. *Rissa* has two."

"You're my exception."

She shook her head and raised her chin. "I'm not *your* anything."

Kyle only smiled, and she imagined he'd perfected the sensuous promise in his gaze years ago. He held her look for a long time, finally asking, "Aren't you going to open your gifts?"

"What did you bring me, anyway?"

"Something I saw that reminded me of you." He handed her the box, smiling a devilish grin. "But I have to warn you, we Harris men are notorious for our ability to give thought-provoking gifts.''

Clarissa slipped her nail beneath the tape, determined to get this over with. Lifting the gift from its box, she raised her eyes. "This is a notorious thought-provoking gift?''

Reacting to her voice, the gift, a plastic flowerpot sporting a plastic flower that was wearing sunglasses and holding a guitar, tawdry-looking from every angle, moved. At her surprised chuckle, it gyrated and appeared to strum its guitar. She laughed all over again.

"I knew you'd like it," Kyle murmured. The flower swooped and swooned to his low, smooth voice much the way her heart did.

"What am I supposed to do with this?" she asked.

"Enjoy it."

She couldn't help but smile at the devilish look that came into his eyes. "All right. Now, what am I going to do with you?''

"I could say the same thing. Enjoy me. But I'm Stef's Christmas gift.''

"Don't encourage her.''

"I'm trying to encourage you. She could always return me. But I'm afraid my parents don't want me back.''

"No doubt." He turned his most devastating grin on her, and Clarissa found herself taking a step back. "Kyle.''

He stepped forward, until she could feel the heat of his body through her sweater. "Kyle," she repeated, this time softer, throatier. She felt his breath on her forehead, and looked up into his eyes.

"Looks like I'm at your mercy. Do what you will.''

"Kyle.''

"Rissa.''

"I mean it.''

"So do I.''

For a moment, Clarissa thought about what he meant her to do with him. Then he was lowering his face to hers, touching his lips to hers, and all thoughts shimmered away. His tongue traced the softness of her lower lip, and his hands, those same hands she'd imagined skimming across her body, slowly slid all the way down her back.

Kyle had thought about kissing Clarissa, had even fantasized about the way her lips would taste and feel beneath his. But never, not even in his wildest dreams, had he imagined she'd respond so completely to his touch.

She was all curves and softness. In the heels she wore even at home, the top of her head didn't reach past his nose. Her fingers had curled into his upper arms, as if she were holding on for dear life. Her head was tipped back, and she moved her lips beneath his in a way that sent his blood pounding through his body. The surge of desire he'd felt the first moment he'd met her was nothing compared to the desire pumping through him now.

She must have felt his desire, too, because suddenly, her back straightened. Instead of kneading his shoulders, her hands pushed against him. She turned her head, breaking the kiss. She took a backward step, and it was all he could do to let her go.

She was pulling away, and it was more than just physically. Searching for a way to ease the transition, Kyle noticed the package he'd dropped to the counter when he'd first taken her in his arms. He reached around her, being careful not to touch her in the process. "Now this one," he whispered, handing her the smaller gift.

"Kyle," she murmured without meeting his gaze. "You shouldn't have done that."

"I already told you that we Harris men are notorious for buying gifts," he insisted, purposefully misinterpreting her meaning. "It runs in the family. My father gave Mom a cruise for Christmas. Didn't Raine ever tell you about the balloon ride Mitch gave her for her birthday?"

Clarissa nodded, but didn't mention the fact that Raine had also told her what else Mitch had given her that day—a skimpy satin teddy. If Kyle was anything like his brother, she wouldn't be the least bit surprised if the package in her hand contained a pair of thong-bikini underwear, or a leopard-print teddy and black lace stockings.

This time she didn't bother to be careful not to tear the paper. She ripped it open and lifted the gift from inside.

She'd been prepared for something tawdry, but not for this. Kyle's gift was far from tasteless. She ran her finger-tips over the mother-of-pearl box, and slowly lifted the lid. A sweet melody she didn't recognize played from the music box as two tiny dancers floated gracefully across a mir-rored platform inside.

"It's beautiful," she murmured, drawing a breath of air through her parted lips. Why should such a thoughtful gift cause her heart to ache?

"There's more."

For a moment, the tune coming from the music box and his deep, dreamy voice smoothed over her like a love song. Her eyes met his, and the moment stretched to two. For an immeasurable span of time, Clarissa forgot about her sense of guilt, and about her hectic schedule. For that moment, she was just a woman, mesmerized by a man's deep voice, soothed by his warmth and entranced by his laid-back charm.

"There's more?" She placed the music box next to the dancing flower, smiling at the contrast, one tacky, the other elegant, silently thanking him for *not* giving her bikini un-derwear. "What else could you have possibly gotten me?"

He delved into the open music box and brought out a small envelope, which he placed in her hand. "Open this and find out."

She opened the envelope and, after removing an oblong certificate, felt her eyes widen. Her heart thudded several beats before settling heavily in her chest. Eyeing the certif-icate, Clarissa wished he'd have given her sexy lingerie, af-ter all.

Kyle couldn't keep the exuberance from his voice as he said, "It's a gift certificate for dance lessons at a studio in Philadelphia."

"I know what it is."

The tone of her voice had gone flat. He didn't understand why. "You said you couldn't dance."

"I know how to dance, Kyle. In fact, I used to be a dancer. That's how I met Stephanie's father. What I said was that I *don't* dance."

Now that he thought about it, that was what she'd said. "Why not?"

She placed the certificate back inside the envelope and handed it to Kyle. "Why doesn't matter."

"It matters to me." He didn't like the tone of her voice, or the stubborn set of her shoulders.

"I don't have time for this."

"You don't have time to explain why a woman as graceful as you, a woman who used to be a dancer, won't dance with me?"

She raised her eyes to his, and the dark emotions he saw there made him regret the harsh tone of voice he'd used. She turned away from him, and a few things began to make sense.

"You won't dance because Stef can't?"

"Shh!" she said. "I don't want her to hear you."

"What does Stef's handicap have to do with you dancing?"

"I loved to dance, Kyle. But I love her more."

Kyle had heard of illogical logic before. He even went so far as understanding hers. "The fact that you no longer dance has no bearing on whether or not she walks, you know."

"It doesn't matter."

"That's like holding your breath to keep yourself safe when you drive through a tunnel."

"Maybe."

Tears gleamed bright in her eyes, and Kyle felt his heart lurch, because he had a feeling he knew what had put them there. She blamed herself for her daughter's handicap. And she was punishing herself by not allowing herself to do something she loved.

He understood the powerful grip guilt could have on a person. He also understood there was nothing he could do or say to take hers away. But he understood something else, too. For Clarissa's sake, Kyle wanted to try.

Chapter Four

Kyle didn't know what else to say. He would have liked to kiss her again, but Clarissa was acting as if that first kiss had never happened. It had happened, all right. He still felt a few of its consequences, on his lips, in his breathing, and elsewhere. In fact, even now, several minutes later, it required incredible willpower to keep his desire banked.

"Thanks for the gifts," she murmured without looking at him.

Her hand shook slightly as she closed the lid on the music box. Kyle opened it again, placing the certificate for dance lessons back inside.

"You're welcome," he replied, wondering what it would take to make her look at him again. "Christmas dinner was wonderful. The company even better."

"Kyle..."

"What are you doing for New Year's?"

"I don't have time for this," she whispered.

"You don't have time for what, Rissa?"

She finally raised her eyes to his. "Time for fun. Time to date. Time to pursue an empty relationship."

That hurt. But looking into her eyes, he knew she was serious. That was the problem. She was too serious. He drew in a slow, steady breath and said, "You know what they say. All work and no play..."

"Makes me a very boring person. I know," she finished for him.

"I was thinking of me. You're not boring. Interesting, intriguing. But never boring."

Clarissa didn't know what to say to that. She'd never met a man more difficult to dissuade. He glanced at his watch and turned toward the living room, all in one motion. The man had nonchalance down to a science. He also had her head spinning.

In the living room, where Stephanie was still sleeping on the sofa, he said softly, "I should be going."

She handed him his coat, then reached down for the skates. He slipped his right arm through one sleeve then took the skates from her outstretched hand and slipped his left arm through the remaining sleeve, all without taking his eyes off her. "You didn't answer my question, you know."

"What question?" she asked on a whisper. She could have told herself she was whispering because she didn't want to wake Stephanie, but she knew that wasn't entirely so. She was whispering because the look in Kyle's eyes lowered her eyelids, because the tone of his voice lowered her own and because it reminded her how she'd felt a few minutes ago when he'd kissed her senseless.

"You didn't tell me what you're doing for New Year's Eve."

His mention of the new year reminded her what this one would bring. The pages in her appointment book flashed through her mind, those filled with meetings with prospective brides and florists and caterers, and appointments for Stephanie's physical therapy.

"I'm working, Kyle."

"You're doing a wedding on New Year's Eve?" At her nod, he continued. "Will you be there the entire evening?"

"I might be."

"New Year's Eve is a time to party, not work."

With his words, she thought about those other pages in her appointment book, the pages left completely empty. All Stephanie's work these past five years, all the physical therapy and worries, all her dreams for her daughter had led them to that block of time the last week in January, when Stephanie would undergo what Clarissa hoped would be her last major operation.

If all went well during that surgery, the New Year would see her daughter walking. That had been Clarissa's single goal for five years, since the day the doctor had placed Stephanie in her arms, since the day she'd cried at the horrible injustice of such a beautiful child having to face life from a wheelchair. Since the first time she'd heard the words *congenital defect,* she'd vowed to do everything in her power to see that Stephanie walked.

No matter how wonderful she'd felt in Kyle's arms, no matter how he exasperated her, no matter how much he drew her, she couldn't give in to this attraction. For Stephanie's sake, she couldn't lose sight of her goal.

"There are other things in life besides fun, you know," she murmured.

He didn't bother with a response to that. "What about later, after the wedding? What are you doing then?" His voice had taken on that satin-sheets-and-moonlight tone again, and for a moment, she pictured him that way.

"You said we're having a party, Mommy. A New Year's Eve party." Both their gazes swung to the little girl trying to push herself to a sitting position on the sofa. "Do you suppose Kyle would like to come?"

It was times like these when Clarissa almost wished her daughter wasn't quite so bright. "I'm sure Kyle has other plans, honey." She shot Kyle a look she hoped he understood.

"Do you have other plans, Kyle?" Stephanie asked.

This time Kyle did stammer for a reply. He watched Stephanie reach for her crutches then push herself to her feet. Minutes ago Clarissa had practically knocked his socks off with her kisses. Now she was shooting him looks that begged him to understand why she wasn't inviting him back.

"Do you?" Stephanie repeated when she'd reached his side. "Amy Jo Parker is spending New Year's in Florida with her grandpa. He has a pool and she says she's going swimming in the winter. I don't care about swimming, but I would like it if you'd come to our party."

Stephanie's mention of swimming brought an image to Kyle's mind, an image of him and his brothers and his best friend, Jason, splashing and playing in the water. The image was so clear he could practically hear Jason's laughter. The memory left a hollow feeling in Kyle's stomach, because that day was the last time any of them had swum in that pool.

"I don't know what I'm going to be doing that night," he answered truthfully, looking from the little girl's round brown eyes, to her mother's.

"Oh." Stephanie replied. "Well, if you're not doing anything, you should come to our party."

Memories of that long-ago day had a way of making Kyle feel raw. Talking about something else—anything else—helped. "What kind of party are you having?" he asked Clarissa.

"It's just going to be Stephanie and me. I promised her I'd rent the latest Disney movie and we'd roast marshmallows over the stove and toast the New Year with mugs of hot chocolate. Nothing exciting."

"Do you wanna come?" Stephanie piped up.

"We'll see," Kyle answered noncommittally.

"Goody!"

Obviously Clarissa wasn't as excited about the prospect of seeing him again as Stephanie was. He couldn't figure that woman out, didn't understand what made her blow hot and cold. The only thing he *did* know was that he wanted to see her again.

Turning to go, he said, "Merry Christmas."

"Merry Christmas," Stephanie called. "Oh, and Kyle? If you come to our party, will you bring my skates, too?"

The door clicked shut behind him, saving Kyle from stuttering through a reply.

There was Christmas music playing from somewhere, but with all the noise everyone was making, Kyle couldn't have said where it was coming from. Wrapping paper was strewn all around the room, the lights on the tree were lit and everyone was there—his parents and Taylor, Mitch and Raine and little Joey. Everyone was practically bursting with Christmas spirit, laughing and kidding and joking. Everyone except Kyle, that is. Not that he was about to let *them* know that.

He took Taylor's needling about their newest bet good-naturedly, but still wasn't committing to anything, certainly nothing as ridiculous as finding a damsel in distress. He made it a point to tell each and every one of his family members what he thought about their Christmas tans.

Mitch, completely besotted with his new wife, had brought a sprig of mistletoe, and Kyle had even taken Mitch's backslap about having no one to kiss in stride. But, if he saw his father kiss his mother, or Mitch steal a kiss from Raine one more time, Kyle was going to come apart at the seams, because every time he saw one of them kiss, he thought about kissing Clarissa. It had been two days since he'd seen her, and he couldn't get her—or her kiss—out of his mind.

Raine and Mitch led Joey off for his nap, and Taylor plopped down on the couch opposite Kyle. "You should have come to Cancun with us, Kyle. I thought I was in love three separate times. I've never seen so many beautiful women in one place. And the bikinis they wore—'' Taylor took a break to breathe ''—would have fit into the palm—''

"Come on, Ed," Mary Harris said to her husband, interrupting her youngest son. "Let's go make a pot of coffee and put the desserts out for later."

Ed Harris winked at his sons and allowed himself to be pulled to his feet. "Don't let her excuse of making coffee fool you. She just doesn't like listening to you *boys* talk about your latest conquests."

"Talk?" she asked. "Brag, is more like it. Besides, if I've learned one thing about raising boys, it's that the more they talk about it, the less they've probably done."

Taylor looked stricken, and Kyle let out his first genuine chuckle of the day.

"What are you laughing about?" his mother asked Kyle. "You've been as quiet as a church mouse all afternoon, and I'll bet my mother's intuition it has something to do with a woman."

Kyle took his turn looking stricken, and Taylor waited until their parents had disappeared into the kitchen before saying, "Why you old dog, you. I flew clear down to the equator for a little action, and you found some right here. So, who is she?"

"Who is who?" Mitch asked, stepping into the room.

"The woman Kyle's seeing."

"Kyle's seeing someone?" Raine asked after letting out a little yelp because Mitch had pulled her onto his lap.

Sickening, Kyle thought. That's what Raine and Mitch were. So happy and so obviously in love they were downright sickening. Raine cocked her head to one side and smiled so softly at Kyle it almost hurt. She was great. Warm and caring and genuine. No wonder Mitch fell in love with her. *Sickening.*

She was also Clarissa Cohagan's new assistant, and Kyle wasn't about to tell Raine about kissing *her* boss. He wasn't about to tell Mitch or Taylor, either.

"There's nothing to tell," he declared. "Besides, I, for one, wouldn't mind hearing more about those bikinis Tay was talking about...."

The afternoon progressed in typical Harris fashion. There was a lot of laughter, a lot of food and a lot of noise. Although he pretended to listen to Taylor's description of the women he'd seen in Cancun, Kyle's mind had been on another woman, one right here in southeastern Pennsylvania.

Hours later, he was the first one to make noises about leaving, and the first one to shrug into his coat and head for the door. "Don't be a stranger," Raine called. "Anytime you feel like pounding a basketball with Mitch, come on over to our place."

He hadn't quite gotten used to the fact that Mitch was married. Hearing Raine say *our place* reminded Kyle yet again of the changes that were taking place within his family. With the gifts he'd received stacked in his arms, he made some noncommittal reply to Raine and once again turned toward the door.

"Hey!" Taylor called. "What are you doing for New Year's?"

Kyle thought about Stephanie's invitation. "I don't know yet. Why?"

"Because the Jorgenson brothers are having a party again this year. They've hired a band and rented a banquet hall with a huge dance floor. Ought to be a great place to win that trophy back from Mitch."

"Win my trophy?" Mitch asked.

"Don't ask," Kyle warned his brother.

"That reminds me," Mary Harris said. "Your cousin Amelia called yesterday and asked me to let all of you know that she and Suzie are planning a surprise sixtieth birthday party for Uncle Martin next month. You know how special you three boys have been to him, how you've helped him keep Jason's memory alive all these years.''

Turning to her new daughter-in-law, Mary continued. "Amelia was hoping you could give her a few pointers on party planning, Raine.''

"Uncle Martin," Raine said. "Is he the one married to Aunt Millie?''

Taylor, Mitch, Ed and Mary all gasped at once. "Bite your tongue, dear," Mary insisted. "Aunt Millie is married to Uncle Joe. Oh, no, I'd never wish Millie on Martin."

"I wouldn't wish her on anyone," Ed grumbled.

As the other members of his family took their turn regaling Raine with horror stories of Millie's tongue-lashings, Kyle finally figured out what had been wrong with him today. It wasn't the mention of Jason. It was something else. Kyle was with his family, yet he was lonely.

With a final goodbye, he turned and strode across the porch and down the steps. He hadn't realized Taylor had followed him until he heard his brother call, "What do you think about the Jorgensons' party? I've heard the band is great, Kyle. And there will be plenty of women to dance with.''

Plenty of women to dance with? Kyle only wanted to dance with one. Turning toward his brother, he said, "I'll think about it, Tay. And let you know.''

"Mommy, that's Kyle's voice!" Stephanie cried. "Why is he on the radio?''

Clarissa placed the rented movie on the seat between her and Stephanie, and turned on the windshield wipers to clear away the gathering snow. Looking behind her, she began to back out of her parking space. "Kyle's voice is on the radio every morning because he works for that radio station," she explained.

"You mean he's famous?''

"His voice is, honey." It was true. Kyle's voice was famous. In fact, the way his low, smooth voice lured the women in Philadelphia and the surrounding area from sleep had won him a plaque naming him the man women wanted to wake up with. His popularity with male listeners was growing, too. He had a way with words and innuendos men could apparently relate to.

Clarissa hadn't meant to set the dial to his station. Now that Stephanie had heard Kyle's voice, she doubted she'd be able to change it.

"Do you suppose he'll come to our party tonight, Mommy?"

Clarissa's heart softened at Stephanie's question. She'd tried to prepare her daughter for the disappointment she'd feel when Kyle didn't come to her party, tried to explain that he was a single man and would undoubtedly have other parties to attend. "I don't think so, Stephanie."

"He said he'd see."

"I know, honey. Adults say that sometimes when they don't know what else to say." Clarissa had read the interest in his eyes on Christmas, and realized he *might* have come if she'd seconded Stephanie's invitation. She couldn't explain why she hadn't, at least not to her five-year-old child.

When they'd neared Allentown, Stephanie said, "Mr. Abernathy thinks he'll come tonight."

Clarissa smiled as she maneuvered the car through traffic. Hadn't she always known her daughter had a strong will? The truth was, Stephanie believed in magic. She believed Mr. Abernathy was Santa Claus and she believed in Christmas wishes. She believed in maybe and what if. And if Clarissa had anything to say about it, she always would.

A few minutes later, she pulled onto a residential street, her eyes searching for the house number of a baby-sitter Raine had recommended. She'd barely pulled into the driveway before a blond-haired teenager popped through her front door and skipped down the steps.

For a moment, Clarissa imagined how Stephanie would look at that age. Her hair would be dark instead of blond, but it would be flying behind her in the cold wind just as Jennifer's was now. She imagined it was Stephanie blithely descending the steps and running toward her, long-legged and graceful. Without crutches, without leg braces.

"Isn't this snow cool? My mom says we haven't had snow like this since I was your age, Stephanie," Jennifer declared, opening the car door and helping Stephanie from her seat with so much ease Clarissa knew she didn't have to worry about the care her child would receive.

Stephanie, completely taken with the teen's exuberance, reached for her crutches and hurried toward the house. Inside, Clarissa gave Jennifer instructions and left a phone number where she could be reached.

"Will you be gone long, Mommy?" Stephanie asked. "Because we can't be late for our own party."

"It's going to be a small, refined wedding, and shouldn't last very long. I just have to deliver the flowers and check on the caterers." Reaching for her daughter's wristwatch, she pointed to the six and the twelve, saying, "I should be back by six o'clock." She brushed a kiss along her child's cheek, then hurried on to the last wedding of the year.

Back home hours later, Stephanie was still bursting with talk of Jennifer. But even talk of her new baby-sitter and their afternoon together didn't keep the little girl from asking about Kyle.

Clarissa did her best to steer the conversation in other directions. They toasted marshmallows and listened to Stephanie's new sing-a-long tape, laughing at how silly the plastic flower Kyle had given Clarissa for Christmas looked swaying and dipping to their voices. By the time they'd watched the animated movie the second time, Stephanie had stopped asking her mother if she *supposed* Kyle was coming.

Studying the watch on her wrist intently, the child sighed. Although she was still a bit unsure about the other numbers, she'd mastered *o'clock* and *thirty*. As near as she could tell, it was ten o'clock, and Kyle hadn't arrived. Peering out the window once more, she said, "I don't think he's coming."

Joining her daughter at the window, Clarissa tried to inject her voice with so much happiness Stephanie would forget all about her disappointment that Kyle hadn't stopped by. "Look, honey. Isn't the snow beautiful?"

It had stopped snowing over an hour ago. The sky had cleared, and now moonlight shone through the trees out front, casting skeleton shadows on the white ground below. "Is it night? Or day?" Stephanie asked.

"It's night. That's the moon reflecting off the white snow."

Childish wonder filled Stephanie's eyes and excitement tipped her voice. "Mr. Abernathy says moonlight on snow brings a special kind of magic."

Clarissa didn't believe in magic, but she did believe in the happiness and excitement in her daughter's voice. She tried not to think about the upcoming surgery, or the pain her child would have to endure. Instead, she pictured her child running and playing. For a moment, she imagined her dancing.

Stephanie yawned, and after a time, Clarissa led her away from the window, taking extra time to brush her fine hair and help her into her long gown and read the little girl her favorite bedtime story. Tucking the blankets up under Stephanie's chin, she kissed her daughter good-night and murmured, "Sweet dreams, honey."

"Mommy?" Stephanie asked when Clarissa had reached the doorway.

"Hmm?"

"If Kyle comes over after I fall asleep, would you ask him to come back tomorrow?"

Glad for the cover of darkness, Clarissa whispered, "People don't stop in this late, honey."

"But if he does, will you invite him back?"

It was a simple request, and Clarissa couldn't think of any way to convince her daughter that Kyle wouldn't come. In this instance, Stephanie would have to see for herself. "All right."

"Promise?"

"Yes, I promise."

Out in the living room, Clarissa straightened pillows and folded Stephanie's sweater. She stacked the plates and glasses from an earlier snack and carried them into the kitchen. Then, turning off all but a lamp in one corner and the lights on the tree, she slipped her shoes off and, tucking her feet underneath her, opened her appointment book to the pages for the upcoming week.

It was eleven-thirty before she looked at the clock again. Closing the appointment book, she returned it, and the notebook now filled with notes, to her desk. She yawned and stretched the crick from her neck. Padding into the bathroom, she scrubbed her face and teeth, then reached to the hook behind the door for her robe and gown.

She checked on Stephanie, remembering her last words of the day, words that had evoked a promise to invite Kyle back if he stopped in tonight. For what had to be at least the millionth time these past five years, Clarissa's heart thudded with an ache and a wish that she could protect her daughter from pain and disappointment.

Leaving the door open only a crack, she cinched the sash of her robe around her waist then wandered out to the living room to turn off the lamp. Shafts of moonlight drew her to the window, and she found herself gazing at the colors of winter. White and silver and midnight blue.

For the past five years, she'd resolutely set about building a new life for her and her child. During the day, Stephanie, hard work and sheer determination had kept loneliness at bay. But on nights like this, when the house was so quiet and the moon so bright, she felt as lonely as the shadows that fell against the snow.

Clarissa stood in the window for a long time, arms crossed, hands wrapped around her ribs. Her mind wandered down no particular path, dwelling on feelings more than thoughts. Somewhere in the old house, a pipe rumbled, and outside a branch periodically brushed against the siding. From down the street, headlights flickered through the trees. Lost in introspection, she stayed at the window, waiting for the car to pass.

Kyle hadn't intended to stop, but he found himself pulling to the side of the street and throwing the lever into Park.

He'd gone to the Jorgensons' party, and Taylor was right, the band was good. Loud and lively. The women he'd danced with were the same way. The last one had made it clear she wouldn't mind *ringing* in the New Year with him. He'd disentangled her arms from around his neck, not even considering her offer. She was attractive and extremely friendly, and Kyle told himself he had no reason to feel moody. But as the minutes dragged by and midnight approached, he'd ducked outside. Alone.

When he'd climbed into his car, he'd had no clear destination in mind. He'd simply pointed his car north and let his thoughts lead the way.

They'd led him straight to Quakertown. Straight to Clarissa.

He'd told himself he was crazy, told himself she'd probably be asleep. He'd reminded himself he had to get up at four to do his early radio show, and told himself he was getting too old to stay out all night. He'd promised himself he'd simply slow down, gaze at her dark windows and keep on going.

But her windows weren't dark. She was silhouetted there. Faint lamplight shone behind her, illuminating wisps of hair around her head and shoulders, casting the rest of her features in darkness. For a long moment, all Kyle could do was stare.

Clarissa came out of her pensive musings slowly. She recognized the red car parked out front, and watched as the light inside the car flickered on and off again. She drew a breath of air all the way to the bottom of her lungs as Kyle closed the door and strode six or seven steps to the sidewalk. The way he stood gazing at her without moving made her heart rate quicken.

The only light outside was moonlight, the only light inside was the dim bulb in the lamp at her back and the colored lights of the Christmas tree in the corner. She doubted any of those had enough illumination to penetrate her face, yet she felt as if Kyle were gazing directly into her eyes.

The wind cut through his hair, and whipped his coat against his body. She pointed to the door, and moved to open it for him. Clarissa didn't know how or why. She only knew that, a moment later, Kyle was standing on one side of the open door, she on the other.

"Hello." That simple word sent her pulse quavering like the swish of a drummer's brush.

"I didn't expect you to stop by tonight."

It seemed to take a great deal of effort to tear his gaze from her mouth. When he finally did, he looked deep into her eyes and said, "I tried not to, Rissa. But I couldn't stay away."

Her thoughts whirled, and she couldn't think of a single reply.

"May I come in?"

She stepped aside, and Kyle stepped in, just barely leaving enough room for her to close the door behind him. "I wasn't sure you'd still be up."

He stood practically motionless only inches away. He smelled as fresh as the winter night, but gazing up into his eyes, she saw something that was far from cold.

"I almost wasn't," she whispered. "I was about to turn out the light." Fighting to come to her senses, she took a step back. Forcing her voice to a level tone and normal volume, she asked, "Why are you here, Kyle?"

Without raising his voice above his original whisper, he said, "Because it's New Year's Eve and I had no one to kiss."

"I assumed you'd have gone to a party tonight."

"I did."

"Then there would have been plenty of women to kiss."

"I only want to kiss you."

Those words echoed through her mind, stealing into her thoughts, chasing away her resistance. She watched, mesmerized, as he stepped closer. And she knew. He was going to kiss her. And she was going to let him.

He leaned forward slightly, his hand gliding down to her elbow. A shiver of want ran through her, making her wonder how her breast would feel cupped in his large hand. His fingers trailed slowly upward, over her upper arm, coming to rest at her shoulder.

Her body reacted to his touch the way the plastic flower had reacted to his voice, swaying, drifting, pulsing to a primitive beat. She hadn't been with a man in a long, long time. Hadn't wanted to or needed to. She wanted to be with Kyle now, and wondered how he did it, how he made her want things, almost need them.

He leaned toward her, his lips parting in invitation. Her eyelids closed drowsily as his lips touched hers. That first taste was as sweet and rich as hot chocolate, and for a long moment she seemed to be floating, engulfed in the sensations flowing through her. Then the kiss changed, deepened in intensity, the room growing darker, her lids heavier.

His lips opened on a breath as if he was surprised by the level of feeling centering at that point of contact. His chin rasped against hers as he drew her closer. He explored her lower lip with his tongue and it was Clarissa's turn to sigh.

His hand trailed from her shoulder, his fingers tangling in her hair. She automatically pressed her face into his palm, moving her mouth over his in the process. Twinkling light flashed behind her closed lids. It could have been from the Christmas tree, or it could have been something else entirely.

Her heart hammered in her chest beneath her breast, and his tongue boldly traced her upper lip and the smooth ridge of her top teeth. His hand finally covered her breast and a sound, deep and sensual and male, escaped him.

There were so many sensations streaking through her body she couldn't concentrate on just one. Every place felt heavy and full, her lower lip, her eyelids, her breasts and another place deep inside her.

She opened her eyes and found herself staring into his, passion-filled and dewy. When his hand moved to her other breast, her lids drifted closed once more. "Oh, Rissa," he murmured, sliding his hands to her back, drawing her fully against him.

Not more than a few moments ago, his clothing had been cooled by the winter wind. Now, she felt only warmth, the kind of warmth an incredibly hot-blooded man emits.

Her desk was in line of her vision, and through half-closed eyes, Clarissa focused on the appointment book she'd placed there a short time ago. That book brought her back to her senses.

Kyle had kissed her, but the kiss hadn't been one-sided. He'd touched her, and her body had responded at every point of contact, and in other places, as well. Her breathing was uneven still, every bit as uneven as his.

"We shouldn't have done that," she murmured, disentangling her arms from around his neck.

It took incredible self-discipline for Kyle to let her go. After meeting her gaze, it took even more. There was a sadness deep in Clarissa's eyes that had nothing to do with the reflection of Christmas lights. He'd seen it before, when she'd looked at Stephanie's leg braces.

"It's late," she declared, moving farther away.

It was the old *there's no hurry but here's your hat* routine. Kyle wasn't accustomed to a woman using it on him. Women asked him when he was coming back, not when he was leaving. Hell, they didn't ask him to leave, not after he kissed them, not after they'd kissed him back. Asking him to leave was usually the farthest thing from their minds.

So why was Clarissa Cohagan doing just that?

He'd had no intention of coming here tonight. Not when the only person who'd invited him had been a five-year-old kid. The memory of the look in Clarissa's eyes when she hadn't seconded Stephanie's invitation to the party had battered his ego all week. He'd told himself a hundred times he didn't go where he wasn't wanted.

For reasons he didn't understand, he'd left the loud party, left a woman behind who'd been more than willing to satisfy his sexual desire. He hadn't even expected Clarissa to be awake, would have been satisfied to gaze at her darkened windows. But her window hadn't been dark. She'd been standing at it, and the light shining behind her had drawn him, nearly as much as the light in her eyes was drawing him now.

"You know what you need, Rissa?" He almost smiled at her expectant look. "Anyone ever tell you that you have a dirty mind?"

"Only you."

For some reason, her words pleased him. *Only you.* He gazed at her beautiful face, noting her kiss-swollen lips and smooth, white skin. Ever so slowly, he let his gaze dip lower.

Clarissa could practically feel the trail his gaze had taken, and for the first time, she became aware of cool air against her skin. The sash at her waist had come undone, and the front of her thick robe hung open, exposing the low neckline of her gown underneath.

Most men would have turned away, at least made a show of not looking. But Kyle Harris wasn't like most men. He wasn't a man to sneak a peek or glance out of the corner of his eye. Oh, no, he wasn't the covert type. He openly stared at her. Up and down and up again.

She didn't flinch beneath his look. How could she when he'd cupped her breasts in his hands moments ago, when she'd responded to his touch, to his kiss, to his passion? How could she flinch when he was looking at her as if she were the most beautiful woman he'd ever seen?

The most beautiful woman he'd ever seen? Clarissa chastised herself for losing her perspective. She knew her priorities, and knew that what he saw and how he made her feel wasn't the most important one. She'd be wise to keep that in mind.

"Are you finished?" she asked, closing her robe and tying it once again. Her words brought his gaze back to hers. She could hear her own heart hammer in her ears as she met the heat in his eyes. There was no doubt in her mind he liked what he saw, no doubt in her mind he'd like to see more.

His gaze lowered, slowly drifting down, over the midnight blue fabric of her chenille robe covering her shoulders and breasts, down past her waist, all the way to her bare feet. Just as slowly, his gaze drifted up again, over every inch of her, finally coming to rest on her mouth.

Keeping her priorities straight had always been simple. She hadn't been tempted to lose sight of them in years. Suddenly, keeping her feet rooted to the floor, keeping her hands from reaching for Kyle, keeping herself from raising up on tiptoe and touching his mouth with hers required more willpower than she'd thought possible.

"Finished?" he asked, finally moving closer. "Oh, Rissa, we're far from finished."

Chapter Five

Clarissa saw his advance coming, and automatically took one step back, another to the side. "Kyle."

"Do you know I love the way you say my name? No one else has ever said it quite that way. Exasperated, perhaps, or teasing, and every once in a while, serious. But honestly, Rissa, never the way you say it."

His words held her spellbound. She turned her head slightly to see his expression, and instantly regretted doing so, because the look in his eyes was so compelling she couldn't look away. No voice that deep, no smile that refined, no words that direct could possibly be as honest as he claimed to be.

His gaze strayed to her hair, and he reached out and took a strand in his hand. She'd touched Stephanie's hair countless times, but it was nothing like the way he was touching hers. Kyle combed his fingers through the hair behind her ear, taking a thick portion and squeezing it within his fist, as if the texture, the thickness and softness were unlike anything he'd ever touched before.

He released her hair slowly, using those fingers to gently draw her chin his way. He moved closer, whispering, "I want you, Rissa."

Clarissa swallowed. "You don't know me."

"I know I want you." She began to shake her head but he interrupted her. "And I know you want me."

"Wanting something isn't always enough."

Kyle had a feeling they weren't talking about the same thing. He took her hand and pulled her hard against him. "Oh, Rissa, you're right. The wanting is only the beginning."

"We barely know each other," she insisted.

Kyle felt his desire for her coursing through him. He also felt the battles taking place inside Clarissa. She wanted him, too. It was there in her eyes, in her sudden intake of breath and in the way she moved against him. But she was fighting her desire with everything she had. Her shoulders were stiff from her silent battle.

He thought about what he knew of the woman in his arms. She was serious and gentle, doling out smiles when he least expected. She was warm and pliant, and he doubted even she knew how sensuous she really was. She was strong-willed, and stubborn enough to give up dancing because her daughter couldn't. If she was stubborn enough to do that, he didn't doubt she was stubborn enough to send him away if he made one wrong move.

And Kyle didn't want her to send him away. He wanted to be with her. Any way she'd let him.

There was something else he knew about this woman. She didn't treat matters of the heart lightly. He had a feeling it had been a long, long time since she'd taken a man to her bed. And double standard or not, Kyle felt an incredible sense of male conceit. She didn't let many people close. She was letting him. He'd have to go slow. But he had a feeling Clarissa Cohagan would be oh so worth the wait.

He dropped his hands from her shoulders and stepped around her to the couch. Lowering himself to the cushion, he casually brought his right ankle to rest on his opposite knee. "What do you want to know?"

Kyle couldn't quite keep a grin from stealing across his face at the way her eyes widened. But he had to hand it to her. She recovered nicely, crossing her arms and shifting her weight to one foot. "What do you mean?" she asked.

"You said you don't know me. Here I am. What do you want to know?"

When she didn't readily respond, he murmured, "Go ahead. I'll tell you anything and everything. Ask away."

She still hadn't said a word, and without waiting for her to tell him exactly what she thought of this conversation, he asked, "What, no questions? Okay, I'll go first."

He watched her perch on the edge of a chair, and for a moment, the way her robe parted to reveal her knee required all his attention. She covered her exposed leg and shot him a knowing look, and suddenly, Kyle forgot what he was going to say.

Ideas gradually formed into words, and anticipation soon followed. "Why don't you start with your favorite color, and your favorite movie," he said.

"My favorite color is blue. Dark, dark blue. And my favorite movie?" She motioned to the tape case lying on the coffee table nearby. "Anything by Disney."

"Disney, huh? Okay. What about your favorite restaurant? Do you like tea or coffee? What kind of music do you usually listen to? How do you feel about disc jockeys in general, me in particular?"

"Are you taking a survey?" she asked.

"You're the one who wanted to talk." He hoped his tone of voice left no doubt to what *he'd* rather be doing.

She gave him a cryptic little snort. "I don't have a favorite type of music, at least not anymore. And my favorite place to eat is at home, because with my work, I eat catered food so often I see it in my sleep."

"In your sleep, huh? Well, now that I've got you in bed, why don't you tell me what you'd like there."

His words didn't embarrass her, or intimidate her. Instead, they seemed to bring out her lightning-quick reflexes, and a secret smile. "That's for me to know, and..."

She didn't finish her statement. She didn't have to. He knew what she meant, and felt tightness coil in his lap at her saucy grin.

With her next statement, the smile disappeared from her lips, but her eyes took on a devilish glint he'd never seen before. "Disc jockeys are fine in general. As far as you're concerned, I prefer tea to coffee, strong and hot."

The woman was amazing. He'd never met anyone who could keep him on his toes the way she did. Kyle felt a lurch of excitement within him as his desire coiled tighter. She liked tea strong and hot. He'd bet his next month's ratings she'd like her lovemaking the same way.

He leaned forward, his gaze dropping to his hands, which brought her foot into his line of vision. She had a small foot, with short toes and a high instep, and he fleetingly wondered if it would feel cold to his touch. He'd touched her there before, at Mitch and Raine's wedding, but then he'd been concentrating more on what was higher. Then he'd wondered how far she'd let him slide that garter, over her foot and ankle, over her calf, past her knee. That time she'd been wearing nylons. This time her flesh was bare.

While his desire was debating with his conscience, she removed the temptation from his reach. She uncrossed her legs and stood, backing toward the door. "It's getting late, Kyle."

He looked at his watch, and followed her up. "That depends on how you look at it. It's only midnight. Happy New Year, Rissa."

"Happy New Year," she replied, taking another step back. She tried to speak, but found herself lowering her voice. "It's too quiet in here," she whispered.

"Turn on the radio. And dance with me."

"I told you. I don't dance."

He lowered his voice even further and stared directly into her eyes. "You won't dance with me. You won't make love with me. Tell me, Rissa. Is there anything you *will* do with me?"

Clarissa felt her eyelids lower, and knew that this time it was more than his voice, and more than his words. He wasn't making any demands; he was simply asking her what she wanted. God help her, because she wanted him.

The look in Kyle's eyes was like a promise, the promise to give her incredible pleasure. She wondered if she dared allow herself to experience that kind of physical satisfaction. He could make her feel beautiful and desirable and infinitely feminine with just one word. Good heavens, how would she feel if she allowed herself to be intimate with this man?

She thought about the promise she'd made to herself five years ago, the promise to do everything in her power to see that her little girl walked. She was keeping that promise. Didn't she always keep her promises? That reminded her of the one she'd made to Stephanie earlier tonight when she'd tucked her into bed, the promise to invite Kyle back tomorrow.

He wanted to know what she *would* do with him. Glancing out the window at the new-fallen snow, she had her answer. "Do you really want to know what I'd do with you?"

He cleared his throat, feigning an offhand interest so poorly she couldn't help but shake her head while she answered. "I'd build a snowman with you."

"A what?"

His question made her smile, and eased the tension in her shoulders. Tipping her head slightly, she repeated, "A snowman. Stephanie's never built a snowman. If you'd like to come back tomorrow morning, you could build one with us."

Clarissa didn't really know what she'd expected, but she hadn't expected his deep chuckle. Nor did she expect the quick brush of his lips against hers, or his carefree words spoken so close to her ear. "I'd love to build a snowman with you. I have to be at the station all morning. Think Stephanie can wait until afternoon?"

"I think so."

"What about you, Rissa. Think you can wait until then?"

"I think I'll manage," she said matter-of-factly.

He didn't let her tone of voice alter his. "Good. Because it's going to be worth the wait. I guarantee it. See you tomorrow afternoon."

Without saying another word, he turned up the collar on his coat. With a male swagger befitting the carefree bachelor he was, Kyle strode through her door.

The only thing poking through Stephanie's purple snowsuit, hat, mittens and scarf the following afternoon was her nose, the same little nose she'd kept pressed to the window most of the morning, waiting for Kyle to arrive. Watching her daughter scooting herself backward across the snow, Clarissa could hardly blame her. She'd been as excited as Stephanie to see him again.

Her daughter's breathless wonder reminded Clarissa of how easy it would be for Stephanie to come to depend on Kyle. That in turn reminded her how deeply her child could be hurt when he eventually left. Clarissa had been about the same age when her father had walked out on her and her mother. Desertion was a harsh word, and an even harsher reality. It had taken her a long time to get over her father's desertion. It had taken a lot longer to get over Jonathan's.

"Are you going to stand around daydreaming or are you going to help us?" Kyle followed his question up with a snowball that plopped to the ground a few feet behind her.

"You, Kyle Harris, are a lousy shot," she replied, turning toward him.

"I'm a lot better at closer range." He was looking at her, and Clarissa saw the double meaning in his words echo in his gaze. The man was incredibly obvious, yet he seemed equally sincere.

"Talk is cheap," she said over her shoulder before going down on her knees near Stephanie to roll the snowman's middle section.

"I'll show you, Rissa, any time you want."

His voice was so low, his words so warm, she was almost surprised the snow didn't melt at his feet. She felt as if she'd been melting ever since last night. Even now, she felt warmed from the inside out, in spite of the cold winter air and the snow beneath her hands and knees.

This wasn't the first innuendo he'd made since his arrival half an hour ago. He'd told her with words, and with the glint in his eye, the depth of his voice and with his fleeting touch. In all those ways, he'd told her that all she had to do was make the first move and he'd take care of the rest.

But Clarissa couldn't make the first move. Not until she was sure Kyle understood. Not until she'd made it clear that she couldn't risk Stephanie's being hurt. She had to make certain Kyle didn't intend to make promises he wouldn't keep, the way Stephanie's father had.

"Kyle," Stephanie called. "The head's all finished."

"Good," he answered. "Just let me push his body your way."

Clarissa gave the ball she was rolling one final shove. With an *oomph*, she gave up moving it any farther. "I don't know how we're ever going to get this one on top of that one," she called.

"Where there's a will there's a way," Kyle declared.

She shook her head slowly, but couldn't help laughing anyway. "You're incorrigible."

"I know."

Stephanie clapped her mittened hands, and Kyle came to help Clarissa move the huge snowball. After a lot of struggle and laughter, they managed to place the snowman's second section on top of the first. Shoulder to shoulder, he said, "See? A perfect fit."

There was a deeper significance in his statement, a challenge and an assurance that he was ready, and willing. The man was wreaking havoc with her nerve endings, as well as her imagination.

"I want to put the head on!" Stephanie declared. "Kyle, would you lift me?"

Kyle looked down at Stephanie's legs as if he was thinking about the braces underneath the purple fabric. Clarissa thought he'd seemed leery around her daughter before. He seemed just as unsure now. But he walked to Stephanie's back and, showing her how to hold the large snowball without breaking it, effortlessly lifted her up. With a shriek of pleasure, the little girl placed the head smack in the center of the larger ball of snow.

For a moment, Kyle looked surprised at how easy lifting her had been. Stephanie clapped her hands, and without warning, twined them around his neck for a quick hug. "Aren't you glad it snowed, Kyle?" she asked.

"Yeah, Stef, I am."

From out of the blue, she asked, "Did you bring my roller skates with you?"

"No, kid, I forgot."

"That's okay. I'm just glad you came back."

He lowered her to the ground as if she were made of crystal, and knelt to help her pack snow around the base of each of the snowman's sections. Clarissa did the same, listening to their chatter.

The man was a study in contrasts. He was obviously leery of kids, but his eyes twinkled whenever Stephanie was near. He'd lifted her into his arms like an old pro, then lowered her to her feet as if he were afraid she'd break. He claimed he waited until the last minute with everything, but always seemed to be on time when he came here. He had the voice of a heartbreaker, but the eyes of a very caring man.

"When my brothers and I were kids, it snowed like this every winter," he said.

"Did you build a snowman every winter when you were little?" Stephanie asked.

"You bet I did. Mitch and Tay and I always built the biggest snowmen in the neighborhood."

"Did anyone else help you?"

When he didn't readily answer, Clarissa peeked around to the side of the snowman where Kyle was packing snow, lost in thought. She doubted he was aware she was watching as he said, "Yeah, Stef, my cousin used to help."

"What was his name?"

"Jason." His voice had dropped almost to a whisper.

"Did you shorten his name like everyone else's?" Stephanie asked.

Kyle had gone completely still. "I used to call him Jase."

"Where is he now?"

Kyle was staring at the white snow, but Clarissa wondered what he was really seeing. "He probably moved away, honey," she told her daughter. But from the look on Kyle's face, she doubted that was true. For a moment, he looked as if he'd lost his best friend, and she had a feeling that once, a long time ago, he had.

Before Stephanie asked any more questions, Clarissa said, "Mr. Snowman is all ready for his face and hat." Hurrying to the front step, she brought back all the items they'd need to finish their snowman.

She handed four big buttons to Stephanie, and with a mischievous smile, held out a huge carrot to Kyle. "Think you can handle putting on his nose?" she asked.

One side of his mouth lifted, slashing that cheek ever so slightly in exactly the way she remembered. Taking the carrot from her hand, he stood, a bright flare of desire igniting the playful gleam in his eyes.

"Just watch me."

The warmth she'd felt inside her all day spread all the way down to her toes. The feeling stayed the entire time it took to put the finishing touches on their snowman: eyes made out of stones, a bright purple scarf and an old straw hat, buttons down the front, licorice shaped into a smile and of course, the carrot nose, which Kyle placed in a way that left little doubt to what he was thinking about.

Clarissa went inside for her camera. After she'd taken several different shots of Stephanie with her snowman, she handed the camera to Kyle and followed her daughter as she rolled away to make snow angels.

While mother and daughter romped and laughed, Kyle watched, and snapped a few pictures. He hung the camera from one of the snowman's spindly stick-arms, and simply stood there watching Clarissa play. The memory of the look in her eyes when she'd handed him that carrot sent blood pumping to his heart. Hearing her throaty laughter as she played with Stephanie, and watching her movements as she made a snow angel set another part of his body strumming with life.

Stephanie was rarely quiet. Although Clarissa seemed oblivious to the endless questions, Kyle marveled at her ability to answer each as it came.

"Do you suppose all snow angels are girls?"

"No, honey. There are boy snow angels, too."

A spurt of playfulness had him bending down to make a snowball or two. With Stephanie's next question, he straightened, holding in his laughter.

"What about snowmen? Do you suppose there are such things as snow-women?"

"I suppose," Clarissa answered, glancing at the snowman they'd just built.

"How can you tell the difference?" Stephanie asked.

Kyle wiggled his eyebrows when Clarissa looked his way, and he couldn't wait to hear her answer.

"Snow-women wear different kinds of hats," she stated matter-of-factly.

With a shake of his head, he mouthed the word *chicken,* and Clarissa cast him a saucy grin and winked before turning her attention back to her daughter. Standing there, Kyle felt a zing go through him, stealing his breath away, making his heart thud and his mind reel.

Thunderstruck. He'd heard the expression. Mitch claimed it had happened to him the first time he saw Raine, but it had never happened to Kyle. Until now. He'd never felt such a pulse-pounding certainty that he'd found his rightful place in the universe. This was where he belonged. With this beautiful woman and her adorable child.

Clarissa found her feet, and brushed the snow from her hair and coat before setting off in Kyle's direction. Several feet away, her steps slowed. She watched as Kyle removed his right glove with his teeth and delved into the pockets of his jeans, which, she noticed, were slightly tighter than they'd been when he'd first arrived.

He placed a piece of hard candy in his mouth and offered her another. With a shake of her head, she cast a glance in Stephanie's direction before asking, "Are you having fun?"

"I've been having fun all day. In fact, there's only one thing I can think of that would be more fun than this. Tell me, Rissa, do you think I pulled my weight in the snowman-building department?"

"I'd say you put in your two cents' worth," she replied with a smile.

"Two cents' worth? I think you'll find I'm worth a little more than that. You might even find that I'm worth my weight in gold." He took a deep breath through open lips and stepped closer. "Get a sitter for Stef and come back to my place with me, and I promise I'll prove it."

It was the word *promise* that sent Clarissa's mind reeling. He'd meant it in a sexual context, and she had little doubt that he could take her to incredible heights of passion. But she knew she wasn't the type to indulge in a one-night stand. She'd want commitment, promises of shared tomorrows, and Clarissa knew better than to believe in men's promises for those.

"You're a very nice man, Kyle. . . ."

Kyle didn't like the sound of that. Not one bit. *Think fast, Harris, before she tells you something you don't want to hear.*

"You're a lot of fun," she continued. "And you already know your list of attributes is long and varied. But . . ."

"Good day, Mrs. Cohagan."

"Mr. Abernathy!" Clarissa jumped, her eyes flickering with surprise to find her neighbor standing directly behind her.

Kyle was surprised, too. Pleasantly. In fact, it was all he could do to keep his relief from pouring out of him at one fell swoop.

Even though he tried to tamp down his gratification at the other man's perfect timing, Kyle found himself pumping Mr. Abernathy's beefy hand in greeting. "So you're Stef's Santa."

Raising one bushy white eyebrow, the old gentleman eyed Kyle. Then, lowering his eyebrow, he said, "It is nice to see you have a new friend, Mrs. Cohagan."

Clarissa took a step toward Kyle, unable to remember the last time she'd forgotten her manners. "Mr. Abernathy, this is Kyle Harris."

"Yes, I see it is."

"Mr. Abernathy! Mr. Abernathy!" Stephanie called from the side yard. The older gentleman waved to Stephanie, bade Kyle and Clarissa goodbye and, hooking his cane over one wrist, slowly made his way toward Stephanie.

When he was out of earshot, Kyle murmured, "He acted as if he already knew me."

"He sometimes says things a little differently than the rest of us," she whispered. "But he's a wonderful man."

"So you don't really dislike men."

Startled by the change in topic, Clarissa looked up, straight into Kyle's dark blue eyes. Those eyes of his smiled a full five seconds before his mouth did. Even so, when his lips moved to reveal the even edge of his teeth and the tiny line that creased one cheek, she wasn't prepared for her body's reaction, wasn't prepared for the subtle softening, swelling, swaying sensation in her chest.

"Of course I don't."

He cast her a knowing smile, and Clarissa was reminded of the first time she'd seen him. That day, she'd thought the glimmer in his eyes said *male on the prowl*. She remembered the way he'd looked this afternoon when Stephanie had asked about his cousin, Jason, and Clarissa had the oddest urge to skim one finger down the line creasing his cheek. Maybe there was more to Kyle Harris than she'd thought.

"Maybe Mr. Abernathy is right, Kyle. Maybe you and I are becoming friends."

"Friends?"

She almost laughed out loud at the trepidation written all over his face. "Yes, friends. I've already told you I don't have time for a relationship. But I don't think anyone can ever have too many friends."

Kyle didn't know how she'd managed it, but before he could form a reply, she'd clapped the snow from her gloved hands, thanked him for helping build their snowman and

told him to stop by again sometime when he was feeling
friendly.

He was left standing there, wondering how in the world
she always managed to stay one step ahead of him, and how
on earth they'd managed to part as friends, when moments
before he'd felt a sensation go through him, a sensation darn
close to love.

"Those are fine angels you've made there," Mr. Abernathy told Stephanie.

Stephanie giggled behind her hand before whispering,
"Kyle came back, Mr. Abernathy. Just like I wished."

"I see, I see. And you like Kyle, yes?"

"Oh, yes. And so does Mommy."

For a moment, Stephanie was mesmerized by the twinkle
in her friend's eyes, and in the way those eyes softened when
he looked at her. "Tell me, child, how can you be sure your
mother likes him?"

"Because she looks at him a lot."

Mr. Abernathy began to chuckle. "And how does she
look at him?"

"She tries not to, but she looks at him like this." Stephanie batted her lashes and gazed up into eyes bluer than the
sky. Before she was through, Mr. Abernathy's chuckle had
grown into full-fledged laughter, belly-deep and infectious.

"I'm afraid the fact that she tries *not* to look at him like
that is cause for concern."

"They're going to fall in love. I just know it."

"Do not put your cart before your horse, child. Love is
not something that can be hurried. You must be patient."

"But he believes in you. He even said."

"And what did he say?"

"I asked him if he believed in Santa, and he didn't change
the subject or anything. He said, 'Doesn't everybody?'"

"Ah, yes, that does sound like Kyle."

"See? He's the one I wished for, the one who believes in Christmas magic."

"I see. Even so, you must remember to be patient. What is it my father used to say? Ah, yes, now I remember. You can't hurry love."

"You can't?"

"I am afraid not, my child."

"Too bad," Stephanie persisted. "Because I just hate to wait."

"But waiting, it is half the fun." Mr. Abernathy rose one bushy eyebrow, cocked his head toward the newly built snowman and chuckled again. This time, Stephanie laughed right along with him.

Chapter Six

Kyle moved the milk, looked behind the juice, and over the top of the cheese and applesauce inside Mitch's refrigerator before he found what he'd been looking for. "Applesauce!" he crowed to Mitch. "You used to hate applesauce."

Kyle removed two beers, handed one to his brother and popped the top of his own can. Mitch took a swig of his beer and shrugged. "Raine and Joey like it and I have to admit, it's not so bad."

After taking another long swallow from the can in his hand, Kyle said, "Maybe improved eating habits is the reason you won two out of three of those games of one-on-one we just played."

Mitch narrowed his eyes and slowly shook his head. "No, I won in basketball because your mind wasn't on the game. What's up, Kyle?"

Kyle didn't answer his brother, younger by barely more than one year, until after he'd followed Mitch up a flight of stairs into the living room of Mitch and Raine's row house in Allentown. "What makes you think something's up?" He swept the pile of blocks littering the center of the chair cushion onto the floor, sat down and cast a look around his brother's cluttered living room.

"Because I know you. You weren't yourself at the Christmas get-together, and you weren't yourself underneath the basketball net tonight. Besides, Taylor was over a few days ago, and he told me about your latest bet, the one involving a damsel in distress."

Pretending to be interested in the basketball game on television, Kyle said, "I never agreed to any bet. Damsels in distress, indeed."

"You know it doesn't really matter who wins Dad's old bowling trophy, at least not anymore. The real trophy is the love of a good woman." After a slight pause, Mitch added, "Are you seeing someone?"

Kyle's gaze finally slid to his brother's, to eyes nearly the same color as his own. "Yes and no."

"What's the matter? She married?"

A buzzer sounded on TV, but Kyle didn't look to see who'd made the foul. "Worse. She wants to be friends."

Mitch laughed out loud, and Kyle cast his brother a nasty scowl. "Nice of you to be so understanding."

"Hell, I understand plenty. If you remember, five months ago Raine wanted nothing more than an adventure. And look how this has turned out. If this woman you're seeing wants to be friends, begin there. Who knows where it could lead."

"You think I might still have a chance with her?"

"I don't know. You haven't told me her name. But what have you got to lose?"

A door opened downstairs, and Raine's and Joey's voices drifted up. "We're home," Raine called.

"We're home," nearly three-year-old Joey echoed, his small feet thumping up the stairs. Seconds later Joey was running toward his father, a huge grin on his face, Raine not far behind. Kyle found himself wishing that Stephanie could take stairs as easily as Joey. More than anything, though, he wished Clarissa would look into his eyes the way Raine was looking into Mitch's.

Begin as friends?

Friends was a far cry from what Kyle wanted to be. He'd been as ready as a randy eighteen-year-old for weeks. And why not? Clarissa Cohagan made him think, she made him curious, and so eager that he could barely see straight. Problem was, she wasn't any more ready for a relationship now than she'd been the first time they'd met. Something held her back, and Kyle was afraid that the something was trust.

Just how did a man go about gaining one very special woman's trust? Maybe Mitch was right. Maybe friendship was the perfect place to begin.

Clarissa automatically looked at her watch when the phone rang. It was ten o'clock; Stephanie had been in bed for two hours, and Clarissa wasn't expecting any calls. So it was probably Kyle. If she'd learned one thing about Kyle Harris these past few weeks it was that he rarely did what she expected.

"This is your friendly disc jockey calling one of his favorite listeners to say hello."

"What makes you think I listen to your station?" she asked, smiling in spite of herself.

"I'm hurt."

Clarissa found herself laughing into the mouthpiece. "No you're not. And just to put the record straight, Stephanie has the radio in the car set to your station. She refuses to listen to anyone else."

"Smart kid."

Clarissa hadn't seen Kyle since he'd helped her and Stephanie build their snowman four days ago, but this was the second time he'd called. The first time, like tonight, she'd found herself laughing as he regaled her with stories of the Harris Boys' antics, as he called them.

The first time, like tonight, she sat down in a comfortable chair, pulled her legs up close to her body and tucked her robe over her feet, settling down for a long, friendly conversation with Kyle. Strains of an old Beach Boys tune filtered across the phone wires, the old music as much a part of Kyle as his deep, compelling voice.

She told him about the doting father of the bride she'd spoken to that morning, and he told her about his station's manager who only wore three-piece suits. By the time Kyle had finished imitating his boss's voice, Clarissa was clutching her aching ribs.

"Oh, Kyle, stop. I'm laughing so hard I'm practically crying. And I never cry."

She heard a moment's pause. "Never, Rissa? Not even when you were a child?"

She'd never met a man who changed topics so quickly. "All children cry, Kyle," she said.

"What did you cry about, Rissa? When you were a child, I mean."

She thought about his question, and remembered all the times she'd cried when she was small. Clarissa hadn't planned to tell Kyle about her childhood, but there was something in his voice that invited her to talk about it. Gazing out the window at the moonlight, she began.

"I was six years old when my father left. He came back once, not to say goodbye to me or to my mother, but to get his things. Just like that, he completely forgot about us."

"I don't think that would be possible. I'd say you're pretty unforgettable."

His words eased the sharp ache in her chest, and she almost smiled. "I know why you're so popular around here. That smooth voice of yours could charm the stripes off an angry tiger."

"I'd rather charm you."

Clarissa heard a buzzing inside her ears and realized it was the blood rushing through her body. The physical awareness between her and Kyle was building, even over the telephone wires. If things had been different, if her father's desertion hadn't put a dent in her belief in men and if Jonathan hadn't squashed it completely five years ago, she might have given in to the attraction. "Fortunately for me, I know better than to succumb to a man's charms."

Kyle didn't know what was going on inside her head. Mention of her father's desertion had changed the tone of her voice. She reminded him of a stray cat, hungry, but not trusting enough to come any closer. And he wanted to get closer. A lot closer.

As the conversation wound around to other topics, Kyle began to understand a few things about Clarissa Cohagan. Of course, he'd heard genuine affection in her voice when she spoke of Stephanie, but it was also there when she talked about Raine, Mitch and Joey, or her mother, and neighbors, even some of her clients. She cared deeply and completely for her friends and family, but she hadn't had a man in her life, not in a long, long time.

She was no man-hater, but somewhere along the way she'd lost her faith in the male half of the species. And Kyle was just the man to give it back to her again.

He heard her yawn, and imagined her sitting in her house, relaxed and comfortable, ready for bed. It was that image that stayed with him after he'd said goodbye and he'd hung up on his end. It was still with him as he hurried into the bathroom where he removed his clothes and stepped into the shower.

Clarissa steered clear of relationships with charming men, she'd said. She wasn't steering clear of him. Oh, she might be telling herself all she needed from him was friendship, but Kyle knew what she really needed—him, a little fun and a large dose of Harris charm.

PLAY

ONE MILLION

ONE MILLION

BIG BUCKS

AND YOU COULD WIN THE

$1,000,000,000.00

PLUS JACKPOT!

SILHOUETTE

YOUR PERSONAL GAME CARD INSIDE...

THE $1,000,000.00 PLUS JACKPOT!

IT'S FREE!

IT'S FUN. BIG BUCKS

HOW TO PLAY

It's so easy...grab a lucky coin, and go right to your BIG BUCKS game card. Scratch off silver squares in a STRAIGHT LINE (across, down, or diagonal) until 5 dollar signs are revealed. BINGO!...Doing this makes you eligible for a chance to win $1,000,000.00 in lifetime income ($33,333.33 each year for 30 years)! Also scratch all 4 corners to reveal the dollar signs. This entitles you to a chance to win the $50,000.00 Extra Bonus Prize! Void if more than 9 squares scratched off.

Your EXCLUSIVE PRIZE NUMBER is in the upper right corner of your game card. Return your game card and we'll activate your unique Sweepstakes Number; so it's important that your name and address section is completed correctly. This will permit us to identify you and match you with any cash prize rightfully yours! (SEE BACK OF BOOK FOR DETAILS.)

FREE BOOKS PLUS FREE GIFTS!

At the same time you play your BIG BUCKS game card for BIG CASH PRIZES...scratch the Lucky Charm to receive FOUR FREE

Silhouette Romance™ novels, and a FREE GIFT, TOO! They're totally free, absolutely free with no obligation to buy anything!

These books have a cover price of $2.75 each. But THEY ARE TOTALLY FREE; even the shipping will be at our expense! The Silhouette Reader Service™ is not like some book clubs. You don't have to make any minimum number of purchases–not even one!

The fact is, thousands of readers look forward to receiving six of the best new romance novels each month and they love our discount prices!

Of course you may play BIG BUCKS for cash prizes alone by not scratching off your Lucky Charm, but why not get everything that we are offering and that you are entitled to! You'll be glad you did.

Offer limited to one per household and not valid to current Silhouette Romance™ subscribers. All orders subject to approval.

EXCLUSIVE PRIZE #   19 4682 53

BIG BUCKS

$

TWO
WAYS
TO WIN
BIG
BUCKS!

HURRY!
*This jackpot
must be claimed!*

Scratch
Here →

LUCKY CHARM GAME!

Claim
4 FREE books
AND a FREE
Mystery Gift!

YES! I have played my BIG BUCKS
game card as instructed. Enter
my Big Bucks Prize number in the
MILLION DOLLAR Sweepstakes III and
also enter me for the Extra Bonus Prize.
When winners are selected, tell me if I've won. If the
Lucky Charm is scratched off, I will also receive everything
revealed, as explained on the back of this page.

215 CIS AQZZ
(U-SIL-R-11/94)

NAME _____

ADDRESS _____ APT. ____

CITY _____ STATE ____ ZIP ____

**NO PURCHASE OR OBLIGATION NECESSARY TO ENTER
SWEEPSTAKES.**

© 1993 HARLEQUIN ENTERPRISES LTD.

PRINTED IN U.S.A.

1. Uncover 5 $ signs
in a row….BINGO!
You're eligible for a
chance to win the
$1,000,000.00
SWEEPSTAKES!

2. Uncover 5 $ signs in
a row AND uncover
$ signs in all 4
corners…BINGO!
You're also eligible for
a chance to win the
$50,000.00 EXTRA
BONUS PRIZE!

THE SILHOUETTE READER SERVICE™: HERE'S HOW IT WORKS

ALTERNATE MEANS OF ENTERING THE SWEEPSTAKES—Hand print your name and address on a 3" x 5" piece of plain paper and send to: "BIG BUCKS", Million Dollar Sweepstakes III, 3010 Walden Ave., P.O. Box 1867, Buffalo, NY 14269-1867. Limit: One entry per envelope.

BUSINESS REPLY MAIL
FIRST CLASS MAIL   PERMIT NO. 717   BUFFALO, NY

POSTAGE WILL BE PAID BY ADDRESSEE

"BIG BUCKS"
MILLION DOLLAR SWEEPSTAKES III
3010 WALDEN AVE.
P.O. BOX 1867
BUFFALO, NY 14240-9952

NO POSTAGE
NECESSARY
IF MAILED
IN THE
UNITED STATES

Standing beneath the spray of the shower, he thought about the first time he'd laid eyes on her at Mitch and Raine's wedding. He thought about the first time he'd touched her, and how she'd looked that night when she'd told him she didn't dance. He thought about the way she'd laughed over the phone tonight, the way her dusky voice struck a chord deep inside him. Too late he realized now was not the time for thoughts like those. He scowled and promptly switched the water to cold.

Kyle's car was parked at the curb when Clarissa and Stephanie pulled into their driveway the next day. By the time Clarissa had helped Stephanie from the car, he was sauntering up the sidewalk, a grocery sack in his arms.

"What's all this?" Clarissa asked after Kyle had playfully tweaked Stephanie's nose and exclaimed over the painting she'd done at school.

"This," he said, eyeing the package peeking out from the top of the bag, "is dinner."

"I see," she said, smiling. "But what is it doing here?"

He placed his free hand over his heart and pretended to be wounded. "I thought I'd cook dinner for my *friends*."

He followed them into the house, explaining, "It's really Tay's fault. He called me at work today to remind me of our standing bet, told me for the hundredth time the place to meet beautiful women is at the grocery store."

He'd placed the grocery sack on her counter, and Clarissa found herself looking into his dark blue eyes. "Have any luck?"

He winked. He actually winked, then said, "No, but I got a great deal on spaghetti sauce."

"Yummy, spaghetti!" Stephanie piped up. "Let's hurry, Mommy, because I'm just starved!"

"All right," Clarissa said to Stephanie. To Kyle, she asked, "So you and your brothers are still betting on that old trophy?"

Without taking his eyes from the ingredients in the sack, he said, "Naw. I told Tay the bet's off. I think it's time to retire Dad's bowling trophy once and for all."

Clarissa felt something give within her chest, something she might have called hope a long time ago. Tonight, she didn't examine the sensation too closely. Tonight, she didn't want to spoil the happy mood.

Once again Stephanie set the table. Once again she kept up a steady stream of conversation. "Amy Jo Parker says her daddy can cook really good. Did you know they named her new baby brother Christopher?"

Before Clarissa could say *yes, honey, you've told me a dozen times,* Stephanie looked up at Kyle, and said "Do you suppose they call him Christopher?"

Kyle, who was in the process of tasting the spaghetti sauce, licked his lips and said, "That's an awfully long name for a brand-new kid. I'd probably call him Chris."

"That's what Mr. Abernathy said, too. Do you suppose Mr. Abernathy likes spaghetti?"

"I suppose most everybody likes spaghetti, Stef," Kyle answered.

"Mr. Abernathy's moving."

"He's what?" Clarissa looked deep into her daughter's eyes.

"He's moving. In a couple more weeks."

"I'm sorry to hear that, honey," Clarissa whispered. "I know what a good friend he's been to you."

"Yeah," Stephanie declared. "But he's still gonna *see me,* you know, when I'm naughty or nice. And I'm going to send him letters, and not just at Christmastime."

Clarissa was amazed at the way Stephanie was handling the news. She'd have thought her daughter's big brown eyes would be spilling over with tears. Instead, she seemed to have accepted his imminent leaving as a fact of life.

Clarissa had been worried Stephanie would become too attached to Kyle, too. Maybe her daughter wasn't as fragile as she'd thought. Maybe her little girl was more adept at handling friendships than *she* was.

A few minutes later, Kyle shooed mother and daughter from the kitchen, and Clarissa went to help Stephanie change out of her good clothes. The smell of something burning had Clarissa scurrying back to the kitchen a short time later.

Kyle stood near the oven, a kitchen towel thrown over his shoulder, a pan of blackened Italian bread sticks held in his oven-mittened hands. "I think your oven might be a little hot," he said gravely.

She swiped the towel from his shoulder and used it to grasp the hot pan. With a flick of her wrist, she'd placed the pan on the stove and pressed the button to turn on the overhead fan. For a long moment, she and Kyle stood shoulder to shoulder, staring as the black smoke billowed toward the exhaust fan.

"Think Amy Jo Parker's father ever burned supper?"

His words drew her gaze, and the subtle look of amusement in his eyes lifted her lips. She started to laugh, and so did he. Before long they were holding on to each other, their chests heaving, their stomachs aching from the laughter bubbling there.

It seemed like a long time before their laughter finally curled away. When it did, Clarissa found herself pressed to Kyle's body, his arms around her back, hers around his. Her face fit the crook of his neck perfectly, and she breathed in his scent.

He smelled good. A little like burned bread, a little like fresh winter breezes. Nothing like any of her other friends.

He was watching her, and Clarissa saw the laughter they'd shared a moment ago still glimmering in his eyes. But she saw something else, too, a tenderness that amazed her. He lowered his face to hers, bringing his mouth down, touching her lips with his, ever so softly.

Kyle went back to his spaghetti sauce as if kissing her so gently, so softly was the most natural thing in the world. "I have an aunt who eats burned toast every morning, but I'm afraid that this bread might be too burned even for Aunt Millie."

She could hear Stephanie's crutches thunking across the living room, and took a small step back, a smile still on her lips. Clarissa nodded her agreement then went about helping Kyle prepare supper, wondering what in the world she used to laugh about before she met Kyle Harris.

"Auntie Raine, what's a brother-in-law?" Stephanie asked the moment Raine closed the door behind her.

Raine, looking radiant in her honeymoon-in-the-Bahamas winter tan, laughed as she stomped the snow from her boots on the rug near the door. "Well, a brother-in-law is either your husband's brother, or your sister's husband."

Clarissa, who was trying to slip Stephanie's arm into her coat and herd her out the door before she could ask another question, wished she hadn't mentioned to Stephanie that Kyle was Raine's brother-in-law. She also wished Stephanie would cooperate instead of watching Raine's every move.

"Why?" Raine asked. "Are you planning on getting married any time soon?"

The child giggled and placed her hand over her mouth. "No, silly. I'm just a little girl. I probably won't get married until I'm old. Maybe when I'm sixteen."

"Twenty-five, at least," Clarissa corrected.

"How old were you when you got married, Auntie Raine?" Stephanie asked.

"Twenty-nine."

"How old is your brother-in-law?"

"My brother-in-law?"

"You know. Kyle."

"How do you know Kyle?" Raine wasn't looking at the child anymore and Clarissa realized the quality that made her friend such a wonderful assistant also made her too astute for her own good.

"I asked for him for Christmas!"

Clarissa eased into her firmest this-is-it voice. "Stephanie asked for a father for Christmas. Kyle just happened along. I've explained to her that we don't receive fathers for Christmas—"

"Mr. Abernathy said," the child interrupted.

"Tell Auntie Raine goodbye, Stephanie."

"Goodbye, Auntie Raine," the child called.

Her friend's laughter followed them down the short hall, and remained in Clarissa's memory while she drove her daughter to her elementary school several blocks away. Raine, on cloud nine and too newly married to realize she might not always be this happy, would undoubtedly tell Mitch, who in turn would probably razz the living daylights out of Kyle. It was probably a good thing Kyle's shoulders were so broad.

Clarissa didn't want to think about Kyle's broad shoulders. Reining in her thoughts, she pushed her memories of Kyle Harris from her mind and concentrated on the week's schedule. After she dropped Stephanie at kindergarten, she drove back to her house where she and Raine went over their list of clients, double-checking their orders and addresses before setting off in different directions. Raine was to meet with a florist here in Quakertown, and Clarissa was to meet with a bride and her mother at an exclusive bridal boutique in Philadelphia, a half hour's drive away.

Several hours later, Raine's voice drew Clarissa's gaze. It was shortly after lunch, and Clarissa and Raine had been working from the office of Weddings, Parties & More in relative silence for a little over an hour. Clarissa slowly brought her eyes into focus, finally removing her hand from the telephone she'd hung up several minutes ago.

"I'm sorry, Raine. What did you say?"

"Never mind what I said. You were miles away just now. Tell me, Clarissa, what do you think of him?" Raine asked in an offhand way.

"Who?"

"Kyle. Or at least I assume it's Kyle who has you staring off into space. Those Harris men have that effect on women."

"Really, Raine. Just because one of the Harris men swept you off your feet doesn't mean we're all susceptible to their charms."

"So, you think Kyle's charming?"

Thoughts of Kyle sent odd sensations through Clarissa's body. "Don't you start in, too. It's bad enough that Stephanie mentions his name a dozen times a day."

"She really asked for him for Christmas?" As always, Raine softened her words with a smile, but there was no disguising the interest in her dark eyes.

"She asked for a *father*," Clarissa corrected.

"But Stephanie's met him?"

"Yes, he helped us build a snowman earlier this week, and last night he burned our supper."

"That sounds like Kyle," Raine said with a smile. "Clarissa, this is wonderful. I'm so glad you're finally dating. But why have you been keeping it a secret?"

Clarissa strove for an even tone of voice as she said, "I'm not keeping it a secret, and I'm not *dating* Kyle, Raine. We're just friends."

"Friends? My brother-in-law, Sexy-voice Harris, is just friends with an attractive woman?"

Clarissa didn't bother with an answer and Raine said, "I guess stranger things have happened. Tell me, Clarissa, how is Kyle with Stephanie?"

Clarissa thought about the way her daughter had wrapped her arms around Kyle's neck when they'd been building that snowman, about the way Stephanie's eyes shone each time she heard his voice over the radio. "Not bad. Why?"

"Really? It's just that he's a little standoffish around Joey. Mitch says he's always been that way around kids. But if you're seeing him and he's good with Stephanie, maybe he's changing."

"I'm not seeing him! Look, Raine, I met him at your wedding, remember? He caught the garter, I caught your bouquet. And then he did the music at another wedding on Christmas Eve and my car broke down, and he drove me home. It was all just a fluke, really. But now we're friends, and I don't plan to ever become more."

"Too bad," Raine answered. "You might have been just the woman to keep that brother-in-law of mine on his toes."

Kyle sat in his darkened bedroom feeling pretty darned good about his progress with Clarissa. For a while there, she'd had him going, had him questioning his prowess where women were concerned. Sure, he never knew what she was going to say next, never knew exactly where he stood with her. But he did know he wanted to be more than *just friends*. A lot more.

He was beginning to think Clarissa wanted the same thing. She just didn't know it yet.

He reached up, adjusting his blinds so that moonlight filtered into his room in long silver slats, wishing Clarissa was here with him. Patience had never been Kyle Harris's long suit, but he was learning. Clarissa was a good teacher.

Kyle knew he was teaching her a thing or two, too. He was teaching her to laugh, teaching her to enjoy life. She'd had him turned upside down and inside out for a while there, when he'd first learned she planned weddings for a living but didn't believe in the institution of marriage.

Now, he was much calmer, much more sure of himself. All he had to do was find a way to prove she was wrong about marriage, wrong about men's staying power in general, his in particular. All he had to do was prove it in the name of friendship.

Kyle had an idea or two. Yessirree. Kyle Harris had a plan.

Chapter Seven

Clarissa heard a slight commotion at the door, but didn't look up from the wedding portfolio she was planning. Moments later, Raine's voice drew her attention. "Clarissa, this package just arrived for you."

Looking up just in time to see a uniformed deliveryman leave the office, Clarissa said, "Go ahead and open it, Raine. It's probably a thank-you from one of our clients."

"I don't think so."

Something in the tone of her assistant's voice drew Clarissa's gaze. A mischievous light danced in Raine's brown eyes as she tucked a strand of chin-length blond hair behind one ear.

"What do you mean?" Clarissa asked.

Raine placed the gift, which felt heavier than it appeared, in Clarissa's hand. "I don't think this is from a *client*," Raine declared, placing the card on Clarissa's desk. "I think you'd better open this one yourself."

Clarissa plucked the silver bow from the package and quickly removed the midnight blue paper. Opening the box, she lifted a heavy object from layers and layers of tissue paper.

"A crystal snowman," Raine exclaimed.

Clarissa cupped the base of the snowman in one hand, and ran one of the fingers of her other hand down the figurine's length. The snowman was about six inches tall and made of solid glass, which accounted for its weight. It was completely clear, except for the nose, an orange carrot. She couldn't look at that carrot-nose without smiling and remembering the snowman Kyle had helped her and Stephanie build last week.

Clarissa picked up the card, and felt her stomach flutter. The tag held her name, and one short line. *Worth its weight in gold.*

"It isn't signed," Raine said.

"No," Clarissa returned.

"But you know who it's from."

Clarissa touched the tiny carrot, and slowly nodded her head. "It's from Kyle."

Raine spun off the desk so fast papers fluttered in her wake. "This is from Kyle? Kyle Harris? Mitch's brother and my brother-in-law?"

Clarissa nodded again.

"Let me get this straight. Stephanie asked for a father for Christmas, and Kyle just happened along. You adamantly told me the two of you are just friends, but he's sent you this gift."

"That's right," Clarissa said.

"Whew," Raine whispered. "Even though *I* think Kyle's pretty great, if you really don't intend to fall in love with him, whatever you do, don't kiss him. A Harris bearing gifts is charming enough. But if Kyle's anything like his brother, his kisses would be absolutely impossible to forget."

Clarissa waited for her heart to stop thudding, waited for the memories of kissing Kyle to drift from her memory.

Then, as dryly as she could manage, she said, "Thanks for the warning, Raine. I'll try to keep it in mind."

The second gift arrived the following morning. Raine was out of the office, and Clarissa signed for the package, which was wrapped in the same colored paper, midnight blue, and topped with a silver bow just as the first one had been.

She carried the package to her desk and sat gazing at it, trying to decide what to do. *Kyle Harris, what are you up to?*

Thinking back to the day they'd built their snowman, she tried to recall his exact words when she'd told him she'd be his friend. Now that she thought about it, she realized he hadn't said anything. At the time, she'd taken his silence as an indication that he understood and agreed that friendship was all they'd ever have. Now she wasn't so sure.

When the first gift had arrived, she'd felt reasonably assured it had simply been a small token reminding her of the snowman they'd built, a kind of parting gift between friends. The second gift's arrival changed everything. This was no longer an innocent gesture. The man was playing games.

She popped off the bow and tore away the paper. This time the card had no inscription, only her name. *Rissa.* He claimed he shortened everyone's name to one syllable, and Clarissa could picture him telling her she should feel honored because he'd left hers at two. The problem was, she did feel honored. And she wasn't sure what to do about it.

She removed a small glass bottle filled to the halfway mark with a clear liquid that looked like water. Several small items were floating in the water: a black hat, what appeared to be tiny black buttons, a pipe and two little stones, and a tiny orange carrot. At the top of the jar were the words *A Snowman In July.* Clarissa shook the jar, and couldn't help smiling at the way the carrot slowly floated to the bottom again.

Still smiling, she realized she'd overreacted. Kyle might have been playing games, but he *was* just being friendly. This second gift proved it.

Raindrops hitting the windowpane drew her gaze, and on impulse, she leafed through the phone book, picked up the telephone and dialed the radio station where Kyle worked. She told the receptionist she preferred not to give her name and was placed on hold for several minutes before Kyle finally came on the line.

"Kyle Harris, at your service." At the sound of his voice something went incredibly soft inside her. He didn't have any idea who was on the other end of the line, but that voice of his was still dreamy enough to reach across the telephone lines, straight to her senses.

"What are you up to?" she asked.

"Rissa."

"I mean it."

"How do you like your snow-people?" he asked.

She wasn't about to give in to the way his words turned her mind to mush. More than anything, she was trying not to give in to the way his voice drew a response from deep within her.

"How did you know it was going to rain and melt all the snow?" she asked in a voice she hoped was less shaky than it felt.

"Years ago I dated the meteorologist who did the weather for the station. I guess some of her expertise must have rubbed off."

"Let me get this straight," Clarissa said. "You've dated a meteorologist, a mechanic, a cheerleader and an astronaut. Is there anybody you haven't dated?"

"I haven't dated you."

She closed her eyes on his words, and at the way they tugged at her heart. "Kyle."

"But then, people don't date their friends, right? So, how are you? What's new?"

Leave it to him to do the opposite of what she expected. "What could possibly be new? It's only been two days since you saw me."

"So you've been keeping track, too. Tell me, Rissa..."

She heard a click, then Kyle's voice was back. "Unless I want my listeners to hear nothing but dead air, I'd better go. Just do one thing for me. Listen to this station tonight at ten forty-eight."

There was another click as the line went dead, and a moment later Clarissa found herself staring at the telephone, wondering how he'd ever managed to get the upper hand. She hung up the phone, eyeing the bottle containing a melted snowman, remembering Raine warning her about Harris men bearing gifts. Kyle was definitely up to something. She'd have to think of some way to convince him to stop.

Kyle had cooked her dinner, but it was obvious he didn't really know her. If he did, he'd know that Clarissa Cohagan was not a woman who played games. He'd know that she had no intention of tuning in to his station at ten forty-eight that night, and no intention of seeing him again in an anything but friendly way. None whatsoever.

Clarissa checked on Stephanie, and breathed a deep sigh that the little girl had finally fallen asleep. Tucking the blanket under her daughter's little chin, she brushed her lips across Stephanie's tear-dampened cheek. Tears stung her own eyes as she tiptoed from the room, and for the first time in a long time, she almost gave in to them.

She hadn't planned to talk about the upcoming surgery until it was nearly upon them, but Stephanie had asked her about it tonight. Clarissa had tried to explain how the doctors would put Stephanie to sleep and *fix* her hip joints so that she could walk.

"I don't want them to fix me," her daughter had replied.

"But, honey, you'll be able to walk without your crutches."

"I can walk with my crutches. Amy Jo Parker thinks they're neat. I can take bigger steps than any of the other kids in my whole kindergarten class. And Mr. Abernathy says everybody's different. Some people need glasses to see, others need to use crutches. He says he has three legs, on account of his cane, and I have four."

"That's true," Clarissa replied with a trembling smile. Stephanie didn't return her smile, and Clarissa didn't know what else to say to convince her daughter this surgery would be a positive step.

"I don't want to go to the hospital, Mommy. Promise you won't make me."

That was one promise Clarissa couldn't make.

Stephanie, who had been blessed with a sunny disposition, rarely cried. But tonight she'd sobbed uncontrollably. She didn't want to go to the hospital. She didn't want any more operations. Clarissa knew her daughter was afraid of pain, of people she didn't know poking her with instruments she didn't like. She'd held Stephanie close, her own eyes clamped shut, her own heart aching with her daughter's pain and fears, until the sobs that shook Stephanie's slender shoulders slowed, and finally stopped.

Shifting the child to the pillow, she tucked Abbie, the plush stuffed animal Kyle had given Stephanie for Christmas, into her arms and smoothed the baby-fine hair away from her daughter's face. Carefully, Clarissa rose from the bed and bent to turn off the lamp. Through the darkness, she heard the catch in Stephanie's voice as she asked, "Do you suppose my daddy would make me go to the hospital?"

Clarissa didn't answer. She couldn't. She couldn't bring the words past the tears at the back of her throat, or past the heaviness centered in her chest. She lowered her eyes, whispering, "Shh. Go to sleep, honey, and I'll see you in the morning." With that, she turned and walked from the room.

It was only a little after nine-thirty, but Clarissa felt physically and emotionally exhausted. It took an iron will to keep the tears at bay while she stood beneath the hot spray of her shower minutes later. After her shower, she wandered out to the living room, but the memory of Stephanie's words caused her determination to falter.

"Do you suppose my daddy would make me go to the hospital?" Those words haunted her. Clarissa would give anything to keep Stephanie from pain, would gladly take her pain if she could. She'd done everything in her power to bring her child happiness, to make her strong and secure and safe. She'd done it all alone. And then, out of the blue, Stephanie had asked if her *father* would do the same. Her *father,* who'd deserted them both, who hadn't even been back once to see his own beautiful child.

Her mind working overtime, Clarissa wandered into the kitchen and took a bottle of soda from the refrigerator, hoping the taste of cola would dissolve the tears that threatened to be her undoing. With slow steps she walked back out to the living room, deep in thought.

She couldn't blame Stephanie for her fear of the unknown, for her fear of pain and needles and hospitals, nor could she blame her for asking about her father. But Clarissa didn't know how to tell Stephanie that of course Jonathan wouldn't force her to undergo surgery. Because Jonathan wouldn't be there when she woke up from surgery, when she took her first steps, just as he hadn't been there throughout the past five years.

Without releasing the bottle of soda, she placed it on her desk, the image of her ex-husband suddenly soaring into her mind. She hadn't thought about Jonathan in a long time, but whenever she did, she always thought of him soaring.

She'd been trying out for a dancing part in an off-Broadway play the first time she met him. He was a photojournalist and, as a favor to a friend, was covering the play. The attraction was instantaneous and mutual, and happened at a time in her life when she thought she could conquer the world.

She landed the small part, and she and Jonathan quickly became a couple. Jonathan Cohagan was an energetic man with dark hair and eyes. He made friends easily, but in the entire time she'd known him, he'd divulged very little of his background. She knew he was an only child, and that his father had died after a long illness years ago, and his mother shortly after. Jonathan had loved Clarissa. To this day, she knew it was true. But she also knew there had always been a part of himself he held back.

Clarissa's first clue that he couldn't tolerate the sight of blood came while she was pregnant with Stephanie, when he'd informed her he wasn't going to be in the delivery room with her. She'd accepted that, although she'd never fully understood it.

He came to see her and Stephanie several times in the hospital, and each time Clarissa had felt chilled to the bone, as if he were flying away, out of her reach. He never held his daughter, although Clarissa was sure she saw love in his eyes the first time he'd seen their baby.

He'd reminded her of a caged eagle the last time she saw him, when he came to her hospital room to tell her of the chance of a lifetime. He had the opportunity to work for a prestigious magazine, to travel the world, to photograph it from every angle. He was going to soar, he'd said.

Then, just as her father had done, he left. He'd said he'd be in touch. A year later, divorce papers had arrived. Like her father, he hadn't looked back.

Like her father, he'd had no staying power, no stamina in grave situations. Like her father, Jonathan just plain hadn't loved her enough, because if he had, he would have come back for her and Stephanie.

Clarissa came out of her musings slowly, and found herself staring at the bottle of soda. *What were men good for, anyway?*

She grasped the bottle in one hand and turned the cap with the other. But it was no use. The skin on her hand was going to give way before the bottle cap ever did. She rubbed the marks the grooves in the cap had left in her skin, and wondered what ever happened to old-fashioned bottle caps, the kind that didn't require a man's strength to open.

Maybe that's what men were good for. They could open tight caps and pry the lids off jars. Isn't that what can openers were for? From somewhere came another thought: Men could make a woman laugh, make her feel cherished. Unfortunately, they could also break her heart. Twice in one lifetime was enough.

She didn't honestly believe a man's sole purpose in life was to open jars. Most of Stephanie's doctors had been wonderful. She knew there were other good men in this world. Mr. Abernathy was one of them.

Kyle was another. The thought came unbidden, yet in her heart, she knew it was true. Kyle *was* a good man. Devilish maybe, and stubborn, but he was kind, too, although she doubted he'd appreciate that description.

Clarissa didn't want to think about men tonight. She especially didn't want to think about how alone she felt, how long and lonely the rest of her life seemed at that very minute.

She'd intended to turn off the lamp, but her eyes automatically settled on the numbers on the digital clock radio on her desk. It was ten forty-seven. Her hand fell away from the lamp's switch, and she turned on the radio instead, adjusting it to Kyle's station just as the seven rolled into an eight.

"It's ten forty-eight, folks," the late-night disc jockey murmured. "I've had an unusual request from a good friend of mine."

Clarissa listened, wondering what Kyle was up to, wondering why he'd asked her to tune in to this station at precisely ten forty-eight.

"This next song is for a special woman."

Clarissa went perfectly still. It was no longer the late-night disc jockey's voice reaching her ears over the air. It was another voice, the voice of the one man in the whole world who could talk her to liquid. *Kyle.*

"Listen, then look into the night."

Listen, then look into the night. The words were still echoing through her mind as the first notes of the song shimmered through the quiet room.

Clarissa felt her eyes close, felt herself sway to the music. She stood there in the dimly lit room, listening to the words of the sweet, old-fashioned love song, her head bowed, her heart pounding, until the last refrain had been sung. *So darlin', save the last dance for me.*

The request, her memories of Jonathan, and of Stephanie's tears, were almost too much for her. She'd never felt so utterly alone, so soul-weary and isolated. Not when her father had left. Not even when Jonathan had.

Halfway through the next song, she turned off the radio and slowly turned around. *Listen, then look into the night.* Those were the exact words Kyle had used.

She didn't know what he was up to, why he'd sent those gifts, or why he'd dedicated that particular song to her when he knew darn well she didn't dance. Whatever his reasons, she wished he hadn't, because hearing that song tonight reminded her of dreams she'd once had.

She hadn't intended to listen, and she hadn't intended to look into the emptiness of the night. But Clarissa walked to her front window and found herself doing just that.

Only the night wasn't empty. Kyle was there, leaning against his car. Arms folded, one knee bent, he gazed at her without moving. Long before her heart had settled back into its rightful position in her chest, he straightened and strode up the sidewalk.

She opened the door before he could knock, and from the light in the hallway, Kyle didn't know what to make of the shadows on her cheeks, or the ones deep in her eyes. He stepped into the room and closed the door against the cold night air.

She gazed up at him without stepping away. "Why, Kyle?"

He wasn't sure what she was asking: Why he was here, or why he'd prerecorded that message and played that song for her. Or was she asking why on a much deeper level?

"What's wrong?" he asked.

Kyle had never seen her like this. She held her shoulders so stiff, her spine so straight, he was afraid she'd shatter if he so much as touched her. She didn't answer his question, but she finally moved, and finally took a deep, shuddering breath.

"Rissa," he repeated. "What is it? What's gotten you so upset? Was it hearing that song?"

She raised her eyes to his then lowered them again, and he didn't know how she managed to keep the tears from falling. "No," she finally said. "It's not the song. It's Stef."

Kyle wondered if she realized she'd just called her daughter by *his* nickname for her. "What about her?"

"She fell apart tonight, cried like I've never seen her cry before."

"What's wrong with her?" he asked, walking closer.

"She doesn't want to go to the hospital. She doesn't want to have the surgery. She wanted to know if I thought her *father* would make her go through with it."

Kyle felt his eyes narrow as her words stopped his forward motion. Mention of surgery or hospitals always had that effect on him. But he wasn't feeling *his* anxiety right now. He felt Clarissa's. *Damn*. That was a new one. He wasn't entirely sure he liked the emotions that cut deep in his chest. But he was absolutely certain he liked the sorrow in Clarissa's eyes even less.

His reasons for playing that song were simple. He'd wanted her to think about him, to want him as much as he wanted her. His reasons for coming here were just as simple. He'd wanted to see her again, to hold her again.

But it hadn't worked out as he'd planned. Clarissa wasn't falling into his arms. She wasn't even chastising him for pursuing a relationship with her. She looked like a woman doing everything she could to keep the dragons in her memories away. Kyle wanted to help her slay those dragons.

He shrugged out of his coat and tossed it to a chair before lowering himself to the couch. Stretching out his legs, he straightened his jeans, then glanced at Clarissa for a sign of objection. Not that he'd let that stop him.

Finally settled, he slanted another long look her way and asked, "Mind if I sit down?"

Clarissa crossed her arms and studied the man making himself comfortable on her living-room couch. His sandy-blond hair was windblown and in need of a trim. His eyebrows were darker than his hair, and arched over eyes a shade lighter than a moonless night. She wasn't sure why he'd requested that song for her, or why he'd stopped by tonight. But he was here, and his presence was soothing, in a way she hadn't expected.

Pulling the front of her robe together, she tucked one foot beneath her and sat in the chair adjacent to the couch, adjacent to Kyle. She brought her other leg up, too, tucking her robe over her knee and covering her bare foot.

"What is it?" he asked. "What's bothering you?"

She continued to smooth her hand across the soft fabric as she whispered, "What if I'm doing the wrong thing? What if the surgery isn't successful, and Stephanie has to go through all that pain for nothing?"

She finally raised her gaze to his, and the expression in his eyes was so compelling she couldn't look away. "Pain is seldom for nothing," he said. "Everyone experiences it, everyone feels it, and eventually, everyone gets over it."

Clarissa knew firsthand that wasn't always true. There were some aches you never forgot. How could she explain this to Kyle, this easygoing bachelor who'd led a charmed life?

"Which would be more impossible to live with?" he asked. "Having Stef's surgery fail, knowing you've done everything within your power to help her, or shielding her from the very pain that could ultimately give her the chance to soar."

The chance to soar. Funny, he'd used the same words she'd always applied to Jonathan. Those words dredged up old feelings, feelings she'd thought long forgotten, feelings she didn't want to deal with tonight.

"For a man who claims to know next to nothing about kids, you're awfully insightful where they're concerned."

He held up his hands in a gesture of denial. "I'm just an innocent bystander."

A muscle worked in his jaw, and after a moment he continued. "I saw Joey fall down the steps at Mitch and Raine's last week. You know how much Raine loves houses with lots of stairs, but because Joey fell, she was ready to change the entire floor plan for the house they're going to build. The kid bounced down three or four steps, cried for all he was worth, then bounced back and ran off to play."

The soft cadence of his voice smoothed over her taut nerves, but it didn't eliminate the twist of worry deep inside her. "What you're saying is kids are pretty tough."

"Tougher than their parents, I think."

"And Raine and Mitch's floor plan?" she asked.

"Still up in the air."

That's where Clarissa's stomach felt. Up in the air. But it was more than just her stomach. She felt as if her entire life were up in the air. For the first time, she realized it had been this way for more than five years. Since Stephanie was born and Jonathan had left.

"What did you tell Stef when she asked if her father would make her go through with the surgery?"

"I didn't say anything. I couldn't."

She couldn't talk about her ex-husband, even after all these years? Kyle didn't like the sound of that. He didn't like it one bit. He'd fallen in love, and dammit, he wanted his love returned. He'd given the matter a great deal of thought, had spent every waking hour planning the moment when Clarissa would realize *he* was what she wanted.

Kyle knew it took two to tango, and knew Clarissa swore she didn't dance. But he'd thought it was because of Stephanie. Now he wasn't so sure.

Her robe had loosened, and his gaze traveled the long column of her neck and the creamy expanse of skin visible above the royal blue edge of her nightgown. He remembered how she'd responded to his kisses on Christmas. He'd been sure that day, sure of his response, and sure of hers. He wouldn't mind a little reassurance now.

Leaning forward, he grasped the armrest of her chair. Lowering his voice to the tone reputed to sweep women off their feet, he prepared to murmur something provocative, something to make her smile. "What would you say if I told you I love you?"

Blood pounded in his brain as he waited for her reply. He'd planned the gifts, he'd planned the song. He'd planned a helluva lot more, but he hadn't planned to tell her he loved her, at least not yet. Now that the words had been spoken, there was no calling them back.

"I'd say don't confuse love with loneliness."

It wasn't what he'd hoped she'd say, but it made him stop and think. Him, with his full life, his job, his parents and brothers and friends, lonely? Yeah, he guessed he was lonely. For her.

"Are you lonely, Rissa?" he asked as his hand slid from the chair to her arm.

She leaned forward, and her robe parted a little more. He could attribute his incoherent thought processes to the fact that the blood in his brain seemed to have made for a place directly south of there, but it was more than that. He wanted her, yes. But he wanted more than her body. Although, gazing at her exposed flesh, he didn't think that would be a bad place to start.

Clarissa felt the heat in Kyle's expression as surely as she felt the heat beneath his hand. He'd asked if she was lonely. Was she? She was experiencing many sensations right now, and although she was no stranger to loneliness, at the moment that wasn't the most powerful of them.

She tipped her head to one side and the tenderness she felt for this man swelled deep in her chest. "You really are sweet, do you know that?"

Kyle grimaced. He'd told her he loved her, and she told him he was *sweet*. Kids were sweet. Kittens were sweet. Men were virile, strong, sexy.

"For crying out loud, Rissa, you sound like my Aunt Millie. Only she usually says it in a voice shrill enough to break the sound barrier."

"You mean you didn't inherit your sexy voice from her?"

"You think my voice is sexy?"

"You know darn well it is. Tell me more about your family."

The last thing Kyle felt like doing was talking about his family. No, that wasn't entirely true. The last thing he wanted to do was leave. In comparison, talking about his family didn't sound so bad.

"What do you want to know about them?" he finally said.

"Oh, I don't know. Raine's told me Mitch has a lot of relatives. I have Stephanie, of course. But my only other relatives are my mother, who lives in Florida, a second

cousin in Texas and two great-aunts up in Vermont. What"
it like to be surrounded by so many family members?''

Kyle leaned back slightly, but he didn't remove his han
from the arm of her chair. What was it like to be sur
rounded by his family? He'd never given it much thought
"Mostly, it's pretty noisy."

"Noisy?"

"Yeah, everyone's always talking at once. My mother wa
an only child, but my father has three brothers and thre
sisters, all of whom married and took the old adage 'g
forth and multiply' quite literally. Consequently, I hav
cousins coming out of the woodwork."

He looked into Clarissa's eyes, and understood why h
loved her. The woman was beautiful, a little mysterious an
different than anyone he'd ever met. And he'd never wante
anyone more.

"So," she cajoled, "you have a large, noisy family."

"You've met some of them. At Mitch and Raine's wed
ding. Remember my Uncle Martin?"

"The man who called me Clara. I see shortening every
one's name is another inherited trait."

He slanted her a slow smile as he said, "I'm just thank
ful Aunt Millie married into the family. You have no ide
what an enormous relief it is to know I don't have to worr
that my children will inherit any traits from her."

She took her hand from the arm of the chair and pulle
her knee up closer to her body. Kyle recognized a protectiv
gesture when he saw one, but didn't understand the reaso
for hers. "It's getting late."

"You always say that, Rissa. It may be late, but I don'
want to leave. Invite me to stay."

"I can't. I thought you understood all we can be i
friends." Clarissa slid her feet to the floor and slowly stood
"I have nothing to offer you, nothing to give. And I can'
use you or take advantage of you."

Kyle wanted to tell her she was wrong. There were a few things she could give him, a few others she could take from him. There were a few ways he wouldn't mind being taken advantage of, as long as they both did the giving, and the taking, together.

But, gazing at her across the room, he knew she was in no frame of mind to hear what he had in store for them. Just like that, she'd gone from warm to cold. One minute they'd been talking about his family, the next she'd closed herself off from him.

"Clarissa Cohagan, you are one complex woman," he said, lifting his coat from the chair where he'd tossed it earlier. "And I haven't quite got you figured out."

"Don't try, Kyle. It isn't worth your time. And while we're on the subject of time, I want to thank you. For everything. For making Stef laugh, and for the gifts. But now you have to stop, Kyle. It's time we put an end to this, once and for all, before any of us get hurt."

Kyle slid into his coat and strode to the door where she was waiting. With his hand on the doorknob, he asked, "What did you think of our song?"

"It isn't *our* song. And it would be best if you didn't dedicate any more songs to me, Kyle, if you just let it be over."

"You should know me well enough by now to know I don't give up easily. That's another trait we Harrises pass from generation to generation. We're a stubborn lot, each and every one of us."

Clarissa took a step back and turned, as if she'd been slapped. Kyle stared at her unreadable expression before finally turning toward the door. He managed to leave her house, managed to drive back to Philadelphia. But he couldn't get the look in Clarissa's eyes out of his mind. He didn't know how he'd done it, but he'd hurt her. For the life of him, he didn't know what he'd said to put that haunted look in her eyes.

He didn't know what he'd done, but he did know he wanted to undo it. How could he, when she wouldn't tell him what it was she kept hidden, what it was she guarded? Kyle didn't like seeing that pain in her eyes, and was determined to discover what had caused it, and what he'd said to remind her of it. Once he knew, he'd find a way to ease that pain from her heart.

That wasn't going to be easy. Especially when she'd just told him goodbye and closed the door behind him as if she'd meant it. She wasn't going to make it simple for him to slay her dragons, because she wasn't going to make it easy for him to see her again.

Chapter Eight

"I'm glad I caught you before you left, Kyle."

With a flick of his wrist, Kyle decreased the volume of the song he'd been reviewing. He didn't, however, straighten his posture or remove his feet from the desk where he'd propped them fifteen minutes earlier. Eyeing his boss, who had just entered the soundproof room, he asked, "What's up, Will?"

William James McKenzie, the station's manager, grimaced, slapped a file on the desk with one hand and slapped Kyle on the back with the other. "Your ratings, that's what are up. And if your ratings are up, so are the stations'. Take a look at those figures," he declared, motioning to the file near Kyle's left hand.

Turning slightly, Kyle pulled the folder closer. "That's swell, Will."

The other man shook his head. "You know, Kyle, I've always hated to be called Will, but you keep raising your ratings, and you can call me any stinking thing you want."

"Come on, Will. The fact that you don't like it is half the fun."

"I'll tell you what *fun* is. Fun is getting a phone call first thing this morning from the station's owner, commending me for my innovative techniques in drawing listeners. I told him this latest gimmick was all yours. I'm telling you, playing an oldies song at precisely ten forty-eight every night was ingenious. But the next time you come up with a fabulous idea, would you mind checking with me first?"

Kyle finally opened the file and studied the graph on the front page. Sure enough, their station was leading in every area, with his morning show pulling in more listeners than any other time slot, and the late-night segment coming in second.

"The listeners' response has been incredible all week long. I've had to open up a phone line for their comments alone. They all recognized your prerecorded voice, and want to know who this special woman is. This is just the impetus I needed. Remember those billboards I ordered last year?"

Kyle, who was having a hard time mustering up much enthusiasm, didn't bother answering. It didn't matter. William McKenzie continued as if Kyle had. "The station's financial backers have finally okayed the expense. The billboards are going up this week. There's a raise in this for you. Now come on. If you're finished in here, lunch is on me."

Kyle finally let his feet drop to the floor. He sat up straighter in the chair and ran his fingers through his hair. "I'll take the raise, Will. But I'll have to take a rain check on that lunch. I'm meeting Mitch for a game of one-on-one."

"Basketball in the middle of January?"

"It's a great tension reliever."

"If you say so." His boss strode to the glass-paneled door, where he turned and said, "Go on, then, take off. And get a haircut while you're at it."

"A haircut?"

"Yes. If you're going to appear on *Good Morning Phil-adelphia* next week, you'll want to look your best."

"You mean you pulled it off?"

His boss narrowed his eyes and nodded. "The strangest thing happened. I got a call from a man claiming he was Santa Claus. He told me one of the guests scheduled to appear next week was about to have an appendicitis attack and wouldn't be able to be on, after all."

Kyle gave Will a sidelong glance and asked, "Santa Claus, you say?"

"The city's full of crazy people but if it means higher ratings for this station, I'd follow a lead from Rudolph the Red-Nosed Reindeer. Anyway, I called the television station, and guess what?"

"The guy couldn't do the show as planned?"

"Appendicitis. *Good Morning Philadelphia* is yours, Kyle."

Will walked through the door, but stopped before it had closed behind him. "Oh, and Kyle? Good luck with that woman."

"What makes you think I need luck?"

"Because you've just gotten a raise, your ratings are sky-rocketing and you're sitting there looking like a lovesick puppy. It's got to be because of a woman. And from the looks of you, she isn't making it easy on you." With that, the other man ran his hand down his fifty-dollar tie, turned, pushed open the door and strode down the long corridor.

The automatic return closed the door without a sound. Kyle stared long and hard and just as soundlessly into thin air. There was a time when a raise and high ratings would have had him gloating. Today, they hardly registered, because today he realized they weren't really important. He hadn't played that song to increase his ratings. He'd played it that first night to remind Clarissa of him. He'd played it every night since for the same reason.

It seemed nearly half the people in Philadelphia had been tuning in to hear him dedicate a special song every night. He felt as if that song was his only connection to Clarissa, and wasn't even certain she'd tuned in after the first time. She hadn't called him at the station or at his apartment. After too many days of silence, he'd dialed her number. She hadn't answered, and he'd left a message on her machine. She hadn't returned his call, and Kyle figured she didn't plan to.

All because he'd told her he loved her.

The woman had wreaked havoc with his ego since the first time they'd met, refusing to dance with him, refusing to date him, refusing to see him. He'd known she was stubborn from the beginning. Stubborn or not, he wanted to see her, to be with her. If she wasn't quite so stubborn she might just realize she loved him, too.

Kyle removed the compact disc and flipped a switch. He stood and rotated the kinks from between his shoulder blades. Clarissa was stubborn, all right, but he respected that. After all, he was a Harris, and each and every one of them had a stubborn streak of their own. His happened to be a mile wide.

Picking up the file his boss had left, he rifled through the first few pages until he came to the agenda for his debut appearance on television. He squinted at the small print then closed the file and squared his shoulders. He had a show to do, and a woman to sweep off her feet. And a helluva lot to accomplish between now and then if he wanted both to be a success.

From their seats Stephanie and Clarissa watched as cameramen checked their equipment. Microphones were tested, and the director conferred with Amanda Kent, the host of *Good Morning Philadelphia*. So far there'd been no sign of Kyle.

Clarissa hadn't planned to tell Stephanie about Kyle's invitation to watch the live show, but her inquisitive child had overheard Raine talking about it and had been so excited about being in the audience, Clarissa simply couldn't say no. Stephanie's surgery loomed on the horizon, and seeing Kyle on TV was the one thing that seemed to take her mind off her fear.

Stephanie clapped right along with everyone else when Kyle was introduced as *Sexy-voice Harris, Philadelphia's very own disc jockey, the man women want to wake up with.*

Kyle walked onto the set, the overhead lighting picking up the gold highlights in his honey-colored hair, delineating the straight set of his eyebrows and the width of his shoulders. He looked into the camera as if he'd been doing it all his life. All Clarissa could think about was the way he'd looked when he'd told her he loved her.

Amanda Kent handled the crowd's enthusiasm like the pro she was. She asked Kyle all the right questions and, five minutes into the one-hour segment, Clarissa understood why the show had been picked up nationally.

"Aren't you glad we came, Mommy?" Stephanie whispered.

Looking at the happiness on her daughter's face, Clarissa smiled and nodded. For the first time in days, Stephanie's eyes glinted with excitement. She seemed to have forgotten about her upcoming surgery, and was in awe of the bright lights, of all the behind-the-scenes activity.

Clarissa listened as Kyle answered a particularly tricky question about his love life, about *that special woman he dedicated his songs to each night.* His slow smile creased one cheek ever so slightly, and Clarissa realized Stephanie wasn't the only one in awe today.

He'd told her he loved her. Good heavens, what was she going to do about that? She didn't want to hurt him, but he wasn't taking no for an answer. She'd never met a man like him, so stubborn, so sexy, so sweet.

During a station break halfway through the show, Kyle noticed Clarissa leading Stephanie toward the rest rooms. His gaze followed Clarissa's progress across the room. Other men were doing the same. With her eye for detail, Kyle doubted she was oblivious to the appreciative glances. She simply, automatically, categorically dismissed them.

He accepted the glass of water from one of the stage technicians and continued to watch Clarissa from afar. She was undoubtedly a very beautiful woman, but somewhere along the way, Clarissa Cohagan had developed a strength of character at odds with the delicate bones in her face and her slender build.

She'd left her hair down today. Brushed off her forehead, it fell in waves around her shoulders. Everything about her spoke of subtlety—the pale brown color of her suit, her makeup, even her jewelry, which consisted of three pearly strands of beads at her neck, and one strand encircling her wrist.

Her double-breasted jacket stopped just below her waist, and her skirt stopped several inches below her knees. The color of her shoes was a subtle basic brown, but her four-inch heels pushed the line at provocativeness. So did the front slit in her skirt that gave him an occasional glimpse of smooth skin slightly above her knees. A light came on behind her, and Kyle half wished she'd have forgotten to wear a slip. But Clarissa Cohagan was thorough, too thorough to forget such a thing. Kyle knew that if he ever wanted to hear her tell him she loved him, he'd have to be just as thorough. Maybe more so.

The cue that the station break was nearly over came just as she disappeared from view. Kyle settled himself into the stage sofa, pleased with the way the morning was progressing. The show was going well, so well he could practically hear his ratings going up. There was one thing that pleased him even more than that. Clarissa had come.

The cameras were rolling again, and once again Kyle found himself fielding Amanda Kent's questions about the women in his life. He happened to glance into the crowd, and saw Clarissa and Stephanie making their way back to their seats.

With raised eyebrows, he cast a beguiling look at Amanda. "Well, there is *one* special lady in my life."

Kyle's statement froze Clarissa's movements. She felt the blood rushing through her head and the next thing she knew, Kyle was sauntering toward her, the camera suddenly zooming in, making Clarissa feel like a fawn trapped in the glare of headlights.

"Mind if Stef sits with me for a few minutes?" Kyle asked.

She must have nodded, because Kyle wrapped his hands around Stephanie's waist and lifted her into his strong arms, carrying her back to the set. For a second there, she'd been positively terrified that Kyle was going to proclaim his love for her on national television. Thank goodness he was more subtle than that.

With relief coursing through her, she stayed where she was, watching from the sidelines. Kyle settled Stephanie on his knee as if he'd held her a hundred times, but Clarissa didn't miss the protective hand he kept on her daughter's shoulder. "This is the special lady I was telling you about," he murmured with a smile.

Amanda adapted to the new guest, and Stephanie, the little showstopper, looked into the camera as if she'd been born to it. "Kyle," she said coyly, "you look just like a movie star."

Clarissa nearly shook her head at the way Kyle preened at the compliment. He glanced her way, and the overhead lights caught in his eyes like moonlight. He turned his attention back to Amanda's questions, but it was a long time before Clarissa's breathing returned to normal.

She was aware of his appeal. So were half the women in Philadelphia. Sure he was compelling in his dark suit. Sure his voice was deep and sexy and as smooth as brown satin. But it wasn't his clothing or his voice that had her heart fluttering like butterfly wings. It was his smile, and the look in his eyes. It was what he said, and what he didn't say. It was the way he looked into the camera, and the way he looked at Stef. *Good Lord, even she was beginning to shorten Stephanie's name.*

Stephanie told Amanda about Amy Jo Parker's new baby brother, and that Kyle had helped her build a snowman. Moments later, in a small voice, she said, "I want to go back to my mommy now," and, in front of at least a million viewers, gave Kyle a hug and a kiss.

Even though Clarissa wasn't the type of woman who cried easily, she found it difficult to see through the wetness suddenly brimming in her eyes. She took her daughter back to their seats, thinking she had the most beautiful child in the entire world.

"Now," Amanda said to the audience, "I know a lot of you women would love to see what Sexy-voice Harris here looks like without a shirt, and thanks to his brothers, I just happen to have a little clip. Roll it, Randy."

Clarissa laughed right along with the rest of the audience as the fifteen-second tape was played. Amanda had said they'd see Kyle without his shirt, and she was right. Only in the tape, Kyle happened to be about ten years old.

Still laughing, Clarissa glanced at the monitor, and for a moment the look in Kyle's eyes chased her laughter away. He was watching the home movie on another monitor, and his eyes had darkened with emotion. He recovered quickly, but Clarissa found herself looking back at the clip, searching for a reason for the glint of sadness in his eyes.

"Want to tell us who those four sexy young men are?" Amanda asked.

"That's me doing the cannonball off the diving board," Kyle answered. Clarissa wondered if she was the only person who heard the deeper tone of his voice.

"Those two on my right are my brothers, who, as of right now, are in big trouble."

"And the other boy?"

There was a moment's silence, a moment so thick, Clarissa wondered why no one else seemed to notice. "That's my cousin Jason."

Amanda changed the subject, and Kyle was back to his old self, answering her questions with something suggestive, something leaning the tiniest bit toward Irish bull. Kyle Harris was a master of evasion, but Clarissa doubted she'd ever forget the look she'd seen in his eyes as he'd watched the home movie. It made her think maybe he hadn't led such a charmed life, after all.

The hour-long show was finally over, and Kyle let out a deep breath, feeling completely rung-out. Doing television was exhausting. From now on, he was sticking with radio.

The audience had clapped and hooted. Kyle had hardly heard. All he wanted to do was find Clarissa and Stephanie, and go home. Before he'd made it ten feet, his boss, clad in one of his many expensive suits, intercepted him.

"Kyle," Will McKenzie declared, "I've just talked to marketing. Viewer response to *Good Morning Philadelphia* is tremendous. As of this moment, your baby blues have graced the televisions in nearly every living room across the country. And the little kid with braces on her legs was great. One of our key advertisers wants to send her and her family to Walt Disney World."

Kyle attributed his slow reflexes to one of two things. It was either exhaustion, or an aftershock to the nerves he was fighting to control. Seeing that home movie of Jason had left Kyle's head throbbing, and the acid in his stomach eating holes through his composure.

Kyle accepted Will's handshake and congratulations, finally disentangling himself from his boss's clutches. By the time he'd made it to the place he'd last seen Clarissa and Stephanie, they were nowhere to be found.

He asked around, and one of the cameramen said, "You just missed them. The little girl was exhausted and the mother took her home. That woman's some looker, huh? And the kid looks just like her. Too bad about her defect. Could have been a beauty someday."

Kyle felt the hairs on the back of his neck bristle as his blood did a slow boil. Of all the insensitive, bigoted remarks. He clenched his fingers into fists and glared at the man who was drinking coffee as if he hadn't said anything the least bit derogatory. It took all the sheer willpower Kyle possessed to force himself to turn and walk away, when what he was itching to do was rearrange the man's face.

Could have been a beauty someday, my eye. That little kid was already beautiful. Besides, she had more personality and intelligence in her little finger than that jerk had in his entire body.

Kyle was halfway across the room before he started to cool off. For the first time, he truly understood the kind of obstacles, both physical and psychological, Clarissa and Stephanie had faced every day for the past five and a half years. No wonder Stephanie's surgery was so important to Clarissa. No wonder Stephanie was so afraid of it.

Clarissa hadn't mentioned Stephanie's fears again, but evidently Stephanie wasn't making the impending surgery easy on her mother. The strain showed in Clarissa's eyes.

Kyle had always known Clarissa Cohagan's emotions ran deep. He'd thought a little fun and a large dose of Harris charm would alleviate her worries. Even the doctors had told Clarissa how important a positive attitude was to the ultimate success of Stephanie's surgery and physical therapy. Kyle wished there was something he could do to help.

Unfortunately, he felt his charm wearing thin. What they needed were days on end of worry-free fun.

Disney World. Will had said one of their advertisers wanted to give Stephanie's family tickets to Disney World. Worry-free fun and Disney World went hand in hand, like peanut butter and jelly, like strawberries and cream. Like he and Clarissa.

Kyle increased the length of his stride and eyed his boss, the wheels of motion already turning in his head. "Will," he began in his most beguiling tone of voice, "about those tickets to Disney World. Think you could get them to me in, say, a couple of hours?"

Kyle had to endure a cunning remark or two from Will, and a lengthy discussion about who was boss, but two hours later William James McKenzie slapped an envelope in Kyle's outstretched hand.

Kyle Harris had just what the doctor ordered.

Feeling as if her head were spinning, Clarissa reached onto the shelf for the second glass then reached into the refrigerator for two bottles of soda. Mr. Abernathy had stopped by earlier, and Raine had called to ask Stephanie how it felt to be a star. Neither of them had made Clarissa's head spin. Kyle had done that. He'd shown up a few minutes ago, so handsome in his dark suit her breath had caught in her throat. At the moment, he was making himself comfortable in her living room, and she was trying to think straight.

Placing a kitchen towel over the palm of her hand, Clarissa deftly unscrewed the tricky little caps and poured the dark, fizzy liquid over the ice in the glasses. She took a glass in each hand and quietly walked through the swinging door.

She stopped just inside the living room, where Kyle was rummaging through her tape collection with apparent distaste. Instead of inserting a tape into the cassette player, he flipped on the radio and tuned in to a rival station. He finally straightened and, as an oldies group sang *do lang do lang do lang,* met her gaze.

He slanted her a half smile, and Clarissa felt her heart slide all the way to her stomach. "Know what's so great about these old songs?"

"What?" she asked.

"All those do-lang-do-lang's and shoo-be-do's. You don't have to think. All you have to do is feel."

He'd worked late and had come straight from the radio station. His hair was mussed, and although he still wore his suit, the tie was missing and the top two buttons on his shirt had been undone. He looked tired, more tired than she'd ever seen him.

"You aren't even going to consider my suggestion, are you?"

While an oldies group harmonized in the background, Clarissa tried to think of a way to let him down gently. "It's a nice thought, Kyle. But I can't."

She'd automatically turned down his offer of a mini-vacation to Walt Disney World in Florida when he'd first arrived, and she'd expected an argument. She'd at least expected him to remind her that she'd told him her favorite movies were anything by Disney, and that *Walt Disney World* would probably be chock-full of *Disney* characters.

As usual, he did the opposite of what she expected. He hadn't argued or tried to talk her into the trip. He'd grown quiet, and although he wasn't angry, she was sure his smile hadn't reached his eyes ever since she'd quietly told him she had wedding receptions to plan and couldn't possibly fly to Florida on a moment's notice.

Clarissa had stepped out of her shoes shortly after tucking Stephanie into bed but she, too, still wore the jacket and skirt she'd worn all day. She, too, felt exhaustion in every muscle.

She placed the soda on a low table, next to the plane tickets Kyle had brought over, and walked closer. "You really are a very sweet man."

"Great. Sweet is exactly the way I want to be described."

Clarissa smiled at his expression, knowing full well that *sweet* was the last way Kyle Harris wanted to be thought of. "You know what I mean," she murmured.

He placed his hand on her shoulder, slowly drawing her closer. "Why don't you show me what you mean?"

Clarissa tucked one hand inside his open jacket, and the warmth of his fingers slowly seeped into the skin on her shoulder. She couldn't forget the way he'd held Stephanie on his lap during the television show, couldn't forget the way he'd looked when she'd told him she couldn't go to Walt Disney World with him.

He really was sweet. Clarissa could think of only one way to show him. She raised herself on tiptoe, her nylon-clad knees touching the smooth fabric covering his. She wound her hands around his neck and placed tiny kisses along his beard-roughened chin. He didn't tolerate barely-there kisses for long before bringing his hand to the middle of her back and moving his mouth over hers.

His kiss was neither hard nor gentle, more searching than persuasive. She'd turned him down, and he wasn't holding it against her. He'd taken his loss like a man. A very special man, the kind of man she could love, if her heart wasn't locked against the emotion.

His other hand slid to her back, drawing her more fully against him. He moved his mouth over hers like a man exploring something precious. There was passion, yes; there would always be passion in Kyle. But she sensed something else tonight, something as elusive as whispers in the wind.

The kiss ended as slowly as it had begun. Their lips parted, and Clarissa felt the heels of her feet touch the carpet. "You must be exhausted after the day you've had," she said quietly.

Kyle shrugged out of his jacket and settled himself on one end of the couch. Clarissa turned down the music, and with the remote control, started the VCR. "Mr. Abernathy taped the show today. Stephanie's already watched herself on TV a dozen times."

Before going to bed, Stephanie had stopped the tape in the middle of the program, and Clarissa started it there. She didn't take the chair adjacent to the couch. Instead, she sank onto a cushion a few feet from Kyle and curled her legs underneath her. Smiling at the way Kyle answered Amanda Kent's questions, she said, "You had the audience in the palm of your hand."

She grew silent as they came to the place where the camera had zoomed in on *her,* remembering how she'd worried that Kyle would put her on the spot in front of all those people. But he hadn't, and she now realized she'd misjudged him.

The camera had captured Stephanie's personality perfectly, and Clarissa found herself laughing out loud at the way the little girl played the crowd. It was Kyle who finally spoke. "She really is a cute kid. Tay even noticed today."

Clarissa didn't turn her attention to Kyle, but kept it trained on the short home video of Kyle swimming with his brothers and cousin. Before the tape had ended, Kyle took the remote control from her and stopped the VCR.

"I've seen enough. How about you?" He stretched his legs out and rotated a kink from the back of his neck. Clarissa searched his face for a sign of teasing, and found none. The man was completely serious. There wasn't a hint of a smile, not in his eyes, not in his lips. This wasn't like Kyle at all.

She'd known Kyle for less than two months, but she remembered a few occasions when she thought there was something pulling at him, a persistent memory he couldn't forget. In the same soft voice she used when Stephanie was sad, Clarissa asked, "What happened to Jason, Kyle?"

Kyle's gaze slid away from hers, to a place somewhere in the distance, or somewhere in his past, Clarissa couldn't be sure. For a long time, he didn't answer. When he finally did, it was in a voice so quiet, Clarissa had to strain to hear.

"He died."

For several seconds, the music in the background was the only sound in the room. Afraid even the slightest movement might break into his private thoughts, she sat statue-still, waiting for him to continue.

In his mind Kyle could still picture Jason Harris's freckled nose and toothy grin, could still hear his infectious laughter. He could still hear the springing of the diving board, the solid smack of Jason's head hitting wood, and the splash his thin body made when he hit the water.

Kyle felt paralyzed all over again, as if he could still see the blood seeping into the water, as if he could still feel Jase's limp body slipping through his hands. Most of all, Kyle could still taste the panic in his throat, and the crippling fear that froze him to the side of the pool.

Chapter Nine

Kyle wasn't sure why he was about to tell Clarissa any of this. Maybe it was because until now she hadn't asked many questions. Maybe it was because seeing that home video of Jason made him realize Clarissa wasn't the only one with dragons to slay. Whatever the reason, he found himself speaking in a voice he barely recognized.

"Jason was our cousin, but he was *my* best friend. His family lived down the block from ours, and we spent nearly every waking moment together. They had a pool in their backyard, we had a tree house in ours. The neighbors in between our houses used to complain that we trampled their grass traipsing back and forth."

Kyle felt himself smile at the memory, and felt the smile slip away. "It had been a hot, humid summer, and we were all swimming, Mitch and Tay, Jase and me. Uncle Martin was watching from the shade when Aunt Kathy called him inside, and even though we could all swim like fish, he said, 'You're the oldest, Kyle. Keep an eye on the others for me.'"

A sense of dread vibrated through Clarissa, growing stronger and more ominous with every passing second as she waited for his next words.

"We were all playing and splashing, like always. Mitch did a cannonball off the diving board, spraying water everywhere. Jase and I scrambled from the pool to do the same. I went in first, and for some reason, Jason didn't wait for me to get out of the way.

"I saw him from the corner of my eye and tried to swim. Before I'd gone far, I looked back, treading water. Jase slipped, his feet sliding sideways on the wet board. His hands flailed the air, and I caught a glimpse of panic on his face as his head came down on the edge of the board. A second later the panic was gone, and one side of his face was streaked with red."

Clarissa didn't know when her hands had flown to her face, or when the tears had begun to stream down her cheeks. All she knew was that Kyle was hurting, and there was nothing she could do to help.

"My mouth must have been open when he came down on top of me and took me under. He was completely limp, and slipped through my hands. I came up choking. Jason didn't come up at all."

For several moments, that was all Kyle said. Clarissa waited, barely breathing. Finally, she whispered, "How old were you, Kyle?"

"I had just turned thirteen."

"And how old was Jason?"

"He was four months younger. Four months, one week and one day."

"Did Jason die in the water?"

"No. I must have been in shock, because I clung to the side of the pool as if I were frozen, but Tay started screaming, and Mitch ran for help. Uncle Martin dived into the pool and brought Jase up. My parents heard Tay screaming and were suddenly there, prying my fingers from the ledge.

"The ambulance arrived and took Jase away. That night, my parents took Mitch and Tay and me with them to the hospital. Kids weren't allowed in intensive care, but I slipped into Jase's room when no one was looking. His head was bandaged, and Uncle Martin and Aunt Kathy were both crying, each holding one of his hands."

Kyle ran a hand through his hair, and Clarissa finally understood why he'd turned slightly green at the merest mention of Stephanie's surgery. He associated hospitals with his best friend's death, a best friend who'd died as a child.

When he spoke again, she was amazed at the intensity in his lowered voice. "Jase was an inch taller than me. He always bragged about it, but I'll never forget how small he looked in that hospital bed. Everything in that room was either white or stainless steel and reeked of disinfectant. I stayed near the door and watched as Jason struggled to take his last breath. Buzzers went off, and to this day I've never forgotten the sound of Aunt Kathy's soulful wail."

Clarissa felt a shudder pass through her and swiped at her eyes. Kyle had become quiet, but he hadn't returned from his thoughts of the past. She gazed at him through her watery eyes, noticing the strain chiseled around his.

He was different tonight. He looked as handsome as always, but there was a weariness about him, as if dredging up old memories had been exhausting both emotionally and physically. He hadn't said a word about his own fatigue. Instead, he'd shown up on her doorstep with three airplane tickets to Walt Disney World. And what had she done? Turned him down cold.

Beneath his sexy half smile and exasperating stubbornness, Kyle was the warmest man she'd ever met. He'd made no demands on her, had only wanted to see her, spend a little time with her. He'd briefly mentioned love, but she didn't believe he'd been serious about that. He wanted her, physically. But there was hardly any crime in that.

Sitting on the couch near Kyle, Clarissa felt the length of the day in every tight muscle. She was tired to the bone, and could barely remember a time when she wasn't. But this was more than a physical kind of weariness. It was an emotional exhaustion that weighted her shoulders, the same emotional burden she'd been carrying single-handedly for over five years.

Tonight was the first time all week that Stephanie hadn't cried herself to sleep because she was afraid to have surgery. Clarissa welcomed the reprieve, but feared it would be short-lived. She eyed the brochure lying on the coffee table and reevaluated her decision. Kyle had handed her those tickets, and she could still hear Raine's voice in her mind warning her about Harris men bearing gifts.

Clarissa had turned him down quickly, and he hadn't argued. At the time, that had surprised her. Gazing at the lines etched in his face and the tired slope of his shoulders, Clarissa was beginning to understand why. Kyle was as tired, as bone-weary as she.

He'd given her many gifts these past weeks, and he'd never asked for anything in return. He'd given her a piece of himself tonight, yet he wasn't asking for anything now. Kyle was an incredibly special man, but for some reason, she'd thought she had nothing to give him. She'd been wrong.

Reaching for the brochure, she slowly brought it close enough to read in the dim light. "When were you thinking of leaving?" she asked as casually as possible.

"What?"

She forced down her smile, and gasped. "Good heavens, the date on this ticket is the day after tomorrow. Let's see..."

Beginning to think out loud, she stood and paced to the kitchen door and back again. "I'll have to go over the O'Connor wedding with Raine, but I'm sure she can handle it on her own. She's handling the details for her sister's wedding and your uncle's party by herself, anyway, so I won't have to go over those. I want to talk to Stef's teacher and surgeon. And I'll have to get our summer clothes out...."

Finally stopping in front of the coffee table, she said, "You know, Kyle, I'm not even sure her clothes from last summer will fit her."

"You mean you're going?" Kyle asked, slowly rising to his feet.

"I guess that is what I mean. January isn't a busy month for weddings, and I'm sure Raine can handle the workload at Weddings, Parties & More for a few days. Stef's doctors have told me laughter would be the best medicine for her. And I'd say we could all use a little vacation, wouldn't you?"

Kyle may have been tired, but he wasn't totally daft. He knew what she was doing. He'd seen the tears glistening in her eyes when he'd told her about Jason's death, and for the first time in all the weeks he'd known her, he'd seen them course down her face. Clarissa claimed she never cried. Tonight, she'd cried for him.

She'd flat-out refused his offer half an hour ago. But the minute he'd told her about Jason, she'd changed her mind. Kyle hadn't finagled these tickets for himself. He'd done it for Clarissa and Stef, because he wanted to give them a little happiness and a lot of fun.

He saw the heartrending tenderness in Clarissa's gaze, and felt his blood begin to warm, feeling a portion of his old self-confidence return. He'd wanted to give her happiness and fun. It looked as if Clarissa wanted to give him the same thing.

That knowledge went quaking through his body like radio waves leaving a tower, pulsing and spreading wider with every passing moment. If love was supposed to be an emotion unrelated to an actual heart, he didn't understand why his was thudding in a heavy rhythm. He did, however, understand the light in Clarissa's eyes, and for the first time in weeks, he felt his hopes soar.

She may not know it yet, but she felt some deep emotion for him. And he'd bet his ratings that that deep emotion was love.

He held her gaze with his own, and slowly sauntered toward her. She watched his advance with narrowing eyes. Just like that, her chin came up, her shoulders went back and she shifted her weight to one foot. Leveling her gaze at his, she said, "I don't want you to get the wrong impression. This doesn't change anything between us, not really."

It sure as hell did. But convincing her was going to be as tricky as a trigger on a time bomb. Right now, Kyle wasn't in the mood to argue. Looking into her eyes, he realized he couldn't do what he *was* in the mood for, either. At least, not yet.

He tilted Clarissa's head with the palm of his hand, and lowered his face to hers. With the barest brush of his lips against hers, he whispered, "The day after tomorrow we're going to fly away together, you and Stef and me. Two days and one night, that's what we'll have. The days will be for all of us. But the night, Rissa . . ."

Kyle let his voice trail away. Her lids dropped, her lashes sweeping her cheeks only to open wide a moment later. The weariness he'd felt all day had miraculously lifted. Walking to his car, he felt downright lofty, and he figured he had good reason. Clarissa might claim she didn't love him, but she wanted, and needed. For now, that was enough, enough to encourage his hopes, and enough to build on for the future.

"Well, kiddo, what's your favorite ride so far?" Kyle asked Stephanie.

The atmosphere all around them was festive. Clarissa propped Stephanie's crutches against the child's chair and took a seat around the umbrella table, watching as Kyle lowered himself into another chair opposite hers.

Stephanie creased her forehead in concentration, and Clarissa smiled when Kyle tweaked her daughter's nose. She realized she'd been smiling at the oddest times all day, and could have attributed it to the swell of activity in the airport early that morning, or to the air turbulence that had rocked the jet shortly before landing. She could have attributed it to the forty-degree difference in temperature between Pennsylvania and Florida. But Clarissa knew the real reason she felt as animated as the Disney characters fluttering throughout the park.

The real reason was sitting across the small table, stretching his feet out inches from hers. The real reason was Kyle, and the slow smiles he'd given her all day, the fleeting touches and warm looks that told her he was enjoying every moment of their time together as much as she and Stephanie were.

Clarissa listened to Kyle and Stephanie's chatter, thinking how incredibly long it had been since she'd had a man in her life. She'd always thought men had a way of leaving when the going got tough. For the first time in over five years, she thought maybe *some* men stayed. Maybe Kyle was the exception to the rule. Maybe.

But what if he wasn't?

"I liked the jungle cruise in Adventure Land," Stephanie said. "But I loved Fantasy Land the best."

"I'm partial to fantasies, myself, Stef," Kyle murmured.

"What did you like the best, Mommy?"

After meeting Kyle's gaze, it was all Clarissa could do to form a reply. She slanted a smile at her daughter, and after much consideration, said, "I liked Peter Pan's flight and I thoroughly enjoyed the Disney Parade. But I think my favorite was It's A Small World."

"Why that one?" Kyle asked in a deep voice.

She unwrapped Stephanie's pizza, then glanced around. Everywhere, there was brightness. The sky, the umbrella tables, the Disney characters, even the tourists' clothing seemed brighter than any she'd ever seen. "Listen," she finally whispered.

Kyle and Stephanie both looked at her, then slowly looked all around. "Hear that?" she asked. "Those people at that table are from Japan and are speaking Japanese. Those over there are from Argentina. To the left they're speaking French, to the right, Spanish. I don't recognize the language the family behind me is speaking, but here *we* are, speaking English. It's as if each of our little tables is our own little world."

"Of course, Mommy," Stephanie declared. "It's the Magic Kingdom."

For the first time in a long, long time, Clarissa was beginning to believe in magic, at least in the kind of magic that had made Stephanie forget about her surgery and had taken the weariness from Kyle's shoulders. Glancing across the table, she saw another kind of magic in his eyes, and in his slow, slow smile, a kind of magic that had nothing to do with the Magic Kingdom, with rides and cruises through places called Tomorrow Land or Fantasy Land or Adventure Land. This was the kind of magic that would lead to a touch, and a kiss, and so much more. It was the kind of magic she wanted to hold on to, at least for one night. If only she dared.

Hours later, after the sun had begun its slow slide toward the west and dipped below the horizon, after they'd watched the brilliant fireworks display and had taken the monorail from the Magic Kingdom to their motel, Stephanie finally said, "I'm tired, Kyle, would you carry me?"

Kyle thought about telling her she was so tired because she'd stubbornly refused to ride in the wheelchairs provided by the park. He also thought about telling her she wouldn't have to rely on crutches in a matter of a few short days, but he didn't want to upset her, not today. He even considered telling Stephanie she was as stubborn as her mother, but he didn't want to upset Clarissa, either.

Instead of saying any of those things, he hunkered down to Stephanie's level and gave her a wink. "How about a piggyback ride?"

He saw Stephanie hand her crutches to Clarissa, and felt the skinny arms encircle his neck. He, who'd always been leery around children, easily grasped the little girl's brace-clad legs and straightened, effortlessly carrying her from the front desk to their connecting rooms on the third floor.

Clarissa unlocked the door with her card key and Kyle followed her through. He crossed the room where he deposited Stephanie on the bed. With a giggle, the child flopped back on the mattress.

"You, young lady, are wearing a little bit of everything you've eaten today. Come on, honey, I'll help you with your bath," Clarissa said softly.

Kyle strode directly to the dresser where Clarissa had placed the card key. Meeting her gaze, he sauntered to the connecting door and deftly unlocked it. Tucking the key into his pocket, he cast his most decadent look over his shoulder.

"I'll just hop in the shower in the next room, unless you'd rather help me, too."

"You're a man, silly," Stephanie declared. "You don't need any help."

Stephanie giggled, and Clarissa looked from her child to the overgrown kid standing in the doorway. He smiled at Stephanie, but when his gaze met Clarissa's, his smile changed.

"Oh, I don't know," he murmured. "I'll take anything I can get."

Clarissa watched him wink at Stephanie, watched his smile play along his lips and watched his eyes slowly grow serious when he looked at her. She'd seen those expressions before, countless times. The little boy in him came out when he grinned, but the man in him came out when that grin trailed away.

As if he realized she wasn't about to respond to his last statement, at least not in the presence of her five-year-old daughter, he turned and sauntered into the next room. Clarissa bustled about, starting Stephanie's bathwater, taking the child's pajamas from her suitcase, thinking about the glint in Kyle's eyes all the while.

She removed the plastic and stainless steel braces from Stephanie's legs, intentionally failing to mention that, in a matter of a few days, Stephanie wouldn't be needing them anymore. Even though they made short work of the little girl's bath, by the time Clarissa had helped her daughter from the tub, patted her skin dry and carried her to the outer room, they both looked up to find Kyle leaning in the doorway. His shower-dampened hair had darkened to light brown, his blue eyes to royal blue.

He stood watching them as if he had all the time in the world. His upper body was bare and his skin had taken on a golden hue from the light of the corner lamp, one side thrown into shadow. He palmed a stuffed basketball he'd bought for Stephanie earlier today, gave it a playful flip, then tucked it at his side along the low-slung waistband of his jeans. It was the honest-to-goodness pose of a man begging for trouble.

Clarissa's heart thumped, then seemed to slide all the way down to her stomach. She cleared her throat, attempting to concentrate on getting Stephanie into her nightgown.

"I can do it myself."

She handed the gown to her daughter, saying dryly, "Nobody told me you'd go through this stage twice."

Kyle was suddenly there, offering to tuck Stephanie into bed, offering to sit with her until she fell asleep, offering Clarissa the use of his shower. At least that's what he offered with his words. With his eyes, he was offering a lot more.

She gathered what she needed from her suitcases and slipped through the connecting door into the next room. Kyle watched her go. Although he paid close attention to Stephanie, he heard the shower in his room come on, heard the faint sounds of water hitting tiles and imagined that same water running down Clarissa's body. His entire body felt heavy and warm, and ready.

"Do you suppose you could teach me how to play basketball, Kyle?" Stephanie asked sleepily. In spite of doing everything in her power to prevent it, she couldn't seem to hold back a huge yawn.

Kyle sank onto the edge of the bed and said, "First thing tomorrow morning."

Stephanie snuggled into the covers, then peered at her bright pink watch. As if she were fifty, instead of five, she said, "My goodness, it's getting late. I don't think I've ever stayed awake this long before." Then, in a more serious voice, she added, "I sure am glad you came along to Disney World with Mommy and me, Kyle."

"So am I, kiddo." He turned off the lamp and tucked the blankets under her chin.

"Kyle?"

"Yes?"

"Will you really sit with me until I fall asleep?"

"Yeah, I really will. I promise." He moved the desk chair next to Stephanie's bed and settled himself comfortably to wait.

"Kyle?" Stephanie asked a short time later.

"Hmm?"

"I love you."

Those three whispered words sent a knot to his throat and an ache to his chest. In a deep, nearly strangled whisper, he said, "I love you, too, kiddo."

Seconds later, he could hear Stephanie's deepened breathing. It took a lot longer for *his* breathing to return to normal. That little scrap of a girl loved him? Kyle had never felt so strong, and so weak at the same time.

She really was a cute kid. Beautiful, really. And smart, too. How many five-year-olds could count by fives and tell time? He'd always been uncomfortable around kids. At least ever since he was thirteen. But Stephanie hadn't seemed to notice. She'd taken his hand and taken hold of his heart. She'd walked him through his wariness, and she couldn't even walk by herself. That kid got to him. But not as much as her mother. Stephanie loved him. Kyle was beginning to believe that eventually, Clarissa would, too.

He sat there in the straight-backed chair, listening as Stephanie drifted into a deeper sleep. There were sounds in the hall, muted footsteps and faint, muffled voices. But it was Clarissa, standing motionless in the doorway that slowly drew Kyle to his feet.

He'd seen that robe before, more than once. Then it had been belted tightly at her waist. Tonight it hung loose over her body, the front edges of material barely touching, hinting at what was waiting for him underneath.

She held her position in the doorway, and at the same time, held his gaze. She turned slightly as he strode through the doorway, his body brushing her robe aside. It swished back into place, but not before he'd caught a glimpse of bare flesh.

They both cast a look into the dimly lit room where Stephanie was sleeping, but it was Clarissa who pulled the door until it was nearly closed. "We're going to have to be quiet," she whispered.

Kyle took her hand, gently pulling her farther into the room. "That isn't going to be easy, Rissa," he murmured. "Because I want you so bad I could scream it at the top of my lungs."

He didn't release her hand as he cast a sweeping glance at the room. The scent of her shampoo hung thick on the steamy air wafting from the bathroom. An old song played softly from the radio. The bedside lamp had been turned to its lowest setting, the bulb casting shadows into darkened corners and across the bed where the spread was turned back invitingly.

She'd thought of everything. Dim lighting, soft music and fluffed pillows. Kyle could only think about her, of claiming her as his own, of loving her, and of her loving him back.

"Kyle, we should talk."

"Later," he said in a voice so low it nearly vibrated against her skin.

Clarissa had always thought Kyle was a unique combination of moonlight and brown satin. She'd pulled the heavy draperies across the windows, obliterating any traces of moonbeams. This room wasn't decorated in browns or satins, but blues and greens. Still, when she gazed at him, she detected moonlight in his eyes. It reminded her of the night when Stephanie had told her there was a special kind of magic in moonlight. At the time, Clarissa hadn't believed in magic. She wanted to believe in magic now. But something held her back. Like a word on the tip of her tongue, or a thought nagging the back of her mind, she didn't understand why she couldn't.

"I haven't done this in a long, long time," she confessed.

"I know."

She felt a smile steal across her lips at his arrogance. "You're awfully sure of yourself," she whispered.

"Shouldn't I be?"

He reached a hand toward her hair, grasping the thick tendrils in his fist, making her glad she'd taken the time to blow-dry all but the last traces of dampness from her long hair. His gaze claimed hers, then slid back to his hand. He slowly loosened his grip, softly tugging his hand downward through her hair, over her shoulder, forward to the center of her collarbone. Spreading his fingers wide, he massaged the base of her throat, then slowly slid his hand down the center of her chest.

With her free hand, the one not clasped in Kyle's firm grip, she glided her palm across his shoulder, across the dips and planes and ridges of his muscled chest. Although her lids had dropped partway down, her gaze hadn't strayed from Kyle's face, where she watched his eyes follow the course his hand was taking over her body.

Clarissa had never felt more beautiful beneath a man's touch, beneath his gaze. She'd never felt more desirable, or half so wanton. Shrugging her shoulders, she let her robe slide down her body and felt the warm material pool around her ankles.

She breathed deeply, vaguely remembering he'd asked her a question. The heat from his hand sent a shuddering warmth all the way through her. "I love the way you make me feel, and even if this is the only night we'll ever have together, I want to believe in magic."

Despite the sultriness of her voice, the hazy sensuality in her eyes, Kyle heard warning bells go off inside his head. She still believed they had no future, nothing beyond tonight. He could have argued, but arguing with Clarissa Cohagan was about as effective as arguing with a brick wall. Kyle had other ways to prove she was wrong. Ways that were infinitely more enjoyable than arguing.

In one forward motion, he had her in his arms, held tight to his body. He heard her soft gasp of surprise, followed by a murmur of pleasure, and felt her arms wind around his back, felt her breasts pressed to his chest, felt his maleness strain against his jeans. Passion pounded the blood through him, and Kyle gave up trying to discern one sensation from another. All he knew was that he had to have her. Here. Now. Forever.

Clarissa felt a shudder pass through Kyle, and felt as if that same shudder passed through her. His hands were everywhere, in her hair, on her shoulders, encircling her waist and gliding down to her hips, to her back where he squeezed and fitted her against the juncture of his thighs.

He kissed her as if he were claiming her mouth, claiming her. She raised on tiptoe to meet his next kiss. His mouth left hers to press a heavy kiss at the base of her throat, and on up to the hollow below her ear. The need for another kiss swirled within her. Grasping his face between both hands, she brought her mouth to his, the savage harmony of their breathing nearly causing her to swoon.

His hands were suddenly at her sides, his thumbs inching closer and closer to the outer swells of her breasts. Clarissa barely breathed as she waited for those hands to encircle her sensitive flesh, letting her breath out in one long sigh when he took them in his large hands.

Her breasts felt heavy and warm as he kneaded and squeezed, then slowly lowered his head, his tongue wetting each hard bud. The tug of his mouth only increased the tug of her desire, and she felt herself gasp for a breath of air.

With a hand on each side of his face, she held him to her, and let her head fall back, her eyes closed. In his own good time, he brought his lips back to hers, kissing her and whispering unintelligible words, sensual words, desire-laden words in her ear, words that almost made her believe in magic.

And then he was leading her to the king-size bed. He sat at the edge, pulling her into the juncture of his jean-clad thighs. Clasping his arms around her back, he slowly leaned backward, taking her with him.

Her desire spiraled through her, desire to feel more pleasure, and the desire to bring Kyle as much pleasure as he brought to her. She'd never realized she possessed a wantonness so strong, so uninhibited. But the warmth of his flesh was intoxicating, the degree of his arousal thrilling. She couldn't disguise her body's reaction. She didn't want to.

She kissed him soundly on the lips, hungrily, open-mouthed. The moan of pleasure that slipped from the back of his throat spurred her on, her whole being flooded with a desire unlike anything she'd ever known.

A sound from the other room stilled her movements. Heart thudding, she froze, listening for the sound again, hoping against hope some other noise had permeated the passion-hazed atmosphere surrounding her and Kyle.

Stephanie cried out again, the high-pitched wail of a frightened child. With her heart in her throat, Clarissa slid from the bed, reached for her robe and practically flew to her daughter's side.

Chapter Ten

Lifting her daughter to her lap, Clarissa crooned unintel
ligible words, comforting words, everything-will-be-all-righ
words against Stephanie's fine hair. It reminded Clarissa o
the first time the little girl had cried herself to sleep, the nigh
she'd asked about her father.

That night Clarissa hadn't known what to say, but in th
days since, Stephanie had asked countless questions abou
her father. And Clarissa found it wasn't as difficult to tal
to her daughter about Jonathan as she'd thought. She'd tol
Stephanie what Jonathan did for a living, what he looke
like, where they'd lived. She'd told her he'd left shortly af
ter Stephanie was born, but she hadn't told her how soo
after it had really been. There were some things better le
unsaid.

"Mommy?" Stephanie asked.

"Hmm?"

"I don't like Tifany Silverstone."

"Who?"

"Tifany Silverstone. She's Amy Jo Parker's neighbor, and she's in the fifth grade. She's mean, and she told me my daddy probably left because I'm *defected*. She said if her mommy ever had a baby like me, she'd leave her at the hospital."

"Then I feel sorry for Tifany Silverstone," Clarissa murmured. "But do you know who I feel even sorrier for?"

"Who?"

"Her mother. Because she can't see past the outside of a person, to the part that really matters."

"Really?" Stephanie asked in a small voice.

"Really. You see, honey, no matter what happens, I'd rather have you than any other little girl in the whole world." Clarissa didn't say any more, and Stephanie closed her eyes, slowly drifting back to sleep.

Easing Stephanie's head back to her pillow, Clarissa tucked the sheet up close to the child's chin. A sound near the doorway drew her gaze, and she found herself looking into Kyle's face.

Only minutes ago, he'd roused her to the peak of desire, with his hands, and with his lips. Her heart had been thudding so hard her head had spun. She'd wanted to call out to him, to tell him how wonderful he was, how strong and virile and undeniably male. But before she could put any of those thoughts into words, Stephanie had woken up, and the moment was lost.

She and Kyle had nearly made love. She could still see the glimmer of passion in his eyes. They'd been close to the point of no return, practically swept away with wanting, and needing. But Stephanie had called out to her, reminding Clarissa of her daughter's needs.

And those needs overrode everything else. Even her own need for passion. *That* was the thought that had been nigling the back of her mind.

"Is she all right?" Kyle asked from the doorway.

Clarissa nodded.

"Then come here."

He saw her head come up, her shoulders go back. It wa a reflex Kyle was coming to recognize. Clarissa assumed tha stance when she was being particularly stubborn.

Clarissa was careful not to touch him as she entered hi room, and Kyle let his breath out on a long, slow sigh Minutes ago she'd abandoned herself to an incredible whir of sensation, taking him with her to a place he'd never gon before. Nothing in the world had mattered except th woman in his arms, the need bursting between them.

Now she was erecting barriers again, but whether sh knew it or not, she was his. He was a white knight, stron; and sure, and she was his damsel.

Without looking at him, Clarissa said, "I guess Steph anie spoiled the mood."

"Oh, I don't know. I don't think it would be difficult t get it back again."

"Kyle." She'd said it softly, but drew the word out t about twenty letters.

Kyle felt himself smile, on his lips, yes, but deep inside hi body, as well. "Come here," he murmured.

"I'm sorry, Kyle. But I don't think that would be a ver good idea. When you touch me, I seem to forget my prio ities. And I need to keep them firmly in order. Stef needs m now, more than she's ever needed me before."

"What do your priorities have to do with making lov with me?" Kyle asked, his eyes narrowing.

She didn't answer, and Kyle found himself whispering "So you just want to forget what nearly happened betwee us a few minutes ago?"

"I think that would be best, yes."

Best? She thought *forgetting* would be best? Kyle kne women and men were different. Hell, that was an unde statement if he'd ever heard one. But he didn't believe the were *that* different. There was no way he'd be able to forg the way she'd felt in his arms, the way she'd smelled, the wa she'd sounded. And he was sure there was no way she coul either.

Unfortunately, Clarissa was just stubborn enough to *think* she could forget it. For now, he'd let her believe it was true.

Forcing a light tone of voice, he ambled toward her. "All right, Rissa. Maybe you're right. Maybe we shouldn't pick up where we left off. Besides, the way we were going, I probably would have completely forgotten about protection, anyway."

She gasped. "Then it's a good thing Stef woke up, because I could never risk another pregnancy, Kyle. I could never take a chance of putting another child through what Stef's been through."

"What are the chances another child of yours would be born with a birth defect?" This was definitely not the kind of conversation Kyle wanted to have with Clarissa, especially not immediately following the kind of passion they'd just shared.

"What were the chances that Stephanie would be born with it, Kyle? No, I'm sorry, but I can't take that risk. I couldn't put another child through that, and I couldn't survive it again on my own."

Kyle felt his eyes narrow, and worked very hard at controlling his voice, keeping the tone light. "You wouldn't be alone if it was my child, too, Rissa."

She looked at him long and hard for several seconds before finally replying. "That's what my father said. It's what Jonathan said, too."

So it came back to that, did it? She'd placed him in the category with her ex-husband and father and planned to leave him there. The hell she would.

In one smooth motion, he struck his hands to his hips and said, "I'm getting tired of that old argument, Rissa. But I happen to love you, so I'll forgive you for it. I also intend to prove you're wrong about men's staying power. If you really don't want more kids, fine, I'll be a father to Stef. There are enough other Harris men to carry on the family name, anyway."

Clarissa was staring at him as if he were a lunatic. Still, he forged on.

"You love me. You're just too stubborn to admit it. It doesn't matter. I'm sticking around for the long haul."

With that, he marched into the bathroom, leaving Clarissa there by the huge bed, her ears ringing, and her heart throbbing with an ache, an almost physical pain that she'd swore she'd never allow herself to feel again.

Clarissa heard the shower burst on, and heard the short-tempered thuds and thunks coming from the small room. It was the first time she'd ever been nearby when Kyle was angry, and the first time anyone had ever told her they loved her as if they were begging her to make something of it.

He loved her. He'd said it before, but she'd dismissed it, had assumed he used the word *love* in much the way some people used the word *like*. Now she realized she'd been wrong. She honestly believed he'd meant what he said. She didn't like the sudden surge of hope the realization gave her, for with hope came vulnerability, and with vulnerability came heartache. She couldn't open herself up to Kyle, because she couldn't open herself up to heartache.

She quietly padded into the adjoining room to check on Stephanie, who was sleeping soundly. Padding back out again, she found herself gazing at her own reflection in the big mirror in Kyle's hotel room.

Memories of Kyle were pure and clear. Memories of the first time she saw him at Mitch and Raine's wedding, memories of him sliding that garter up her leg, memories of his arriving on her doorstep on Christmas morning, his arms stacked high with presents. Memories of building a snowman together, memories of building passion together. He'd told her he loved her before. Why hadn't she listened? Instead of ending their relationship, she'd agreed to come with him to Disney World.

From the first moment she met him, she'd thought she'd be able to keep him at arm's length. Instead, she'd ended up in his arms. She'd thought she could keep him low on her list of priorities, but he'd risen near the top. That's why she'd come here with him.

Because she cared about him, because she'd seen the sadness in his eyes over his cousin's death. Because she'd recognized his sense of guilt, she'd agreed to fly off to Disney World with him. But she hadn't done it for him alone. She'd done it for Stephanie, too, and for herself, because she'd wanted to briefly live in a magic kingdom, where dreams came true every day.

From the beginning, she'd tried to concentrate on her dream for Stephanie, her dream that her child would walk. After meeting Kyle, it was difficult to concentrate on only one dream. With him, she was in over her head.

She'd thought if she kept him out of her home, she could keep him out of her heart. But he was in her home. He was in the stuffed toy Stephanie slept with every night. He was in the voice she listened to over the radio. He was everywhere—in her car, on billboards, in the snowman figurine in her office, in the silly dancing flower on her dresser. He was in her memories, and now he was in her heart.

The thought froze in her brain. In her reflection she saw her hand fly to her mouth. She loved him. She couldn't even blame him for sneaking into her heart when she wasn't looking. She'd gone into this relationship with her eyes wide-open.

And he'd still taken her by surprise.

Clarissa wasn't sure why she didn't march right into that bathroom, right into his shower and tell him how she felt. She wanted to. But something held her back. The reason had to do with her father, and with Jonathan, and with never having said goodbye. They'd both claimed they'd loved her, yet they'd still left. She couldn't rid herself of the fear that, if she gave in to her feelings for Kyle, it was only a matter of time before he left, as well.

Instead of rushing into his bathroom, she waited until she heard him turn off the shower. Pacing the room, she tried to think of some way to tell Kyle she was sorry, tried to think of some way to tell him she couldn't offer him a permanent place in her heart or in her future.

She turned at the sound of the bathroom door opening. Kyle stepped into the room wearing only a low-slung towel, and a disturbing expression.

"Do you always take two showers a day?"

He didn't smile, but she hadn't really expected him to. Instead, he leveled his gaze at her and said, "I needed some time to think."

"Kyle—"

"Look," he interrupted. "Maybe I overreacted. You don't owe me anything, not even an explanation. You told me from the very beginning that Stef is your first priority. I respect that, although I don't mind telling you I'd like to share the top rung with her."

She started to argue, but Kyle rushed on. "The truth of the matter is this. We came to Florida to have fun, to escape our worries for a few short days. So far, I'd say the trip has been a success, wouldn't you?"

"We can't ever fully escape our worries, Kyle."

"My next point exactly. We have one more day before reality intrudes. We both know Stef's surgery is going to be an ordeal. And I'm going to have to find a way to get through Uncle Martin's party a couple of days later. For now, how about calling a truce?"

In the background, a slow song softly sounded in the quiet room. It was a song Clarissa had come to recognize, the lyrics sweet and moving. *So, darlin', save the last dance for me.* It was the first song Kyle had dedicated to her over the radio, and now, like then, it left her feeling hollow.

Clarissa shifted her weight to one foot, trying to weigh the whole structure of events that had led them here, to this hotel room, to Kyle's last statement. The man standing before her wasn't backing down. He wasn't calling back his terms of endearment. But he wasn't demanding anything, either. He wasn't even asking her to dance.

They had one more day before they had to return to reality, to Pennsylvania and her work and Stephanie's surgery. One more day, and Clarissa didn't want to waste it. He wanted to hold his worries at bay until reality intruded? She wanted the same thing.

Slowly extending her right hand, she said, "You want a truce? It's a deal."

He took her hand in his, and deftly tugged her closer. With her weight unevenly distributed, she easily toppled into his arms. He bent his head, his tongue tracing the soft fullness of her lips. It was the last thing she'd expected him to do. When would she learn to expect the unexpected from Kyle Harris?

Kyle heard her short gasp, her startled cry as his lips touched hers. Rather than prolonging the kiss, he slowly straightened, letting his arms drop from her body, barely managing to grab the towel before it slipped from his hips.

He would have preferred to linger, to shed the towel and make love to her all night long. But a truce was a truce. A deal was a deal. Besides, he was beginning to realize a few things about Clarissa Cohagan. She'd had him going around in circles for weeks. Whether she knew it or not, those circles always led back to her.

Emotionally, she'd been painfully bruised when her father had deserted her as a child. When her husband did the same thing nearly twenty years later, the bruises became scars. Clarissa had good reason to doubt men's staying power. Kyle was just the man to prove her wrong.

"No, Mommy. No. It's gonna hurt. Don't make me, don't make me, don't make me."

A medical technician was leaving Stephanie's room as Kyle entered. Kyle tucked the large box under his arm and took a deep breath. Already feeling slightly green around the gills, Stephanie's wails weren't helping. He looked at the child lying in the hospital bed, trying not to think about another time, when he'd seen Jason lying in a similar bed.

Mustering more enthusiasm than he felt, he said, "Hey, kiddo, what's the problem?"

Two sets of huge brown eyes turned to him, one spilling tears, the other threatening to. Kyle usually liked a woman who was a bit flustered. They had a way of making him feel big and strong and masculine. Clarissa was flustered, and he didn't like it one bit. He didn't feel strong. He felt inadequate. No, he didn't like it when Clarissa was flustered. He didn't like it any better when Stephanie was.

"Guess who I saw in the parking lot?" he asked the little girl.

"Who?" she asked in a quavering voice.

"Your neighbor. He's out there right now trying to park his sleigh."

"You saw his sleigh?" Stephanie asked around a hiccup.

"I don't know if it was really a sleigh. Are they made by Buick?" Kyle asked with a wink. "I have to admit, this one was shiny and red and big enough to be a sleigh. But I'm pretty sure Mr. Abernathy was driving a car, a 1972 model. He was looking for a parking space, a big parking space, when I came in."

Stephanie and Clarissa both smiled in spite of themselves.

"I brought you something," he declared, placing the box next to Stephanie. "Go ahead, open it."

With a sob and another hiccup, Stephanie began to tear the paper from the package. There were actually two packages. One contained a child's board game, the other the skates Kyle had given Stephanie for Christmas, the ones she hadn't been able to use because of her leg braces.

"If this surgery is a success, Stef, you'll be able to use these skates, not just try them on," Kyle promised.

In a rare act of defiance, Stephanie shoved the skates off the bed.

Footsteps sounded in the doorway, and a cane tapped a warning on the metal bed frame. "My, my, child. You owe Kyle an apology, yes?"

Clarissa turned as Mr. Abernathy ambled around to the other side of the hospital bed. "Mrs. Cohagan, Kyle, might I have a moment alone with my friend?"

Casting a worried look at her daughter's face, Clarissa was prepared to turn down her neighbor's request. "Do not worry, Mrs. Cohagan. I would not harm a hair on Stephanie's head. There is something I must tell her, but I am afraid it is for her ears alone. I will only be a moment."

Kyle reached for Clarissa's hand and tipped his head toward the door. He led her from the room and pulled the door closed behind them. Feeling as if he were operating on automatic pilot, it took a moment for him to realize Clarissa had placed her hand on his arm.

"You feeling all right?" she whispered.

There was a sourness in the pit of his stomach, but Kyle managed to keep it there. "I'm fine. How about you?"

"I'll be glad when this day is over."

"You aren't the only one," he replied.

This was the day they'd all been dreading, Clarissa, Stephanie and him. All for different reasons. All for a similar reason, too. Until today, Kyle had never realized that fear came in so many different forms. It was there in Stephanie's understandable fear of pain, in Clarissa's weighted dread and helplessness over her child's pain and the unknown outcome of the surgery and in Kyle's unexplainable fear that history might repeat itself.

They'd all put their fears out of their minds while they were in Walt Disney World. It was hard to believe they'd ever spent two idyllic days in Florida. After their truce, the second day had been even more wonderful than the first. The colors had seemed brighter, the sky bluer, the rides more enchanting.

Out of Clarissa's and Stephanie's hearing, an elderly gentleman from England had complimented Kyle on his beautiful *family*. At first, Kyle hadn't understood why he hadn't set the man straight. As the day had progressed, the reason became clear. It was because he loved Clarissa and

Stephanie. It was because he was beginning to think of them as his family. It was also because he felt it was only a matter of time before his wish would come true, and he, Clarissa and Stephanie *would* be a family.

They'd flown back into Philadelphia at eight-thirty the night before last. That same night, Stephanie had cried herself to sleep all over again.

Clarissa was worried sick. Kyle didn't blame her. But he also knew she was doing the right thing. Stephanie deserved every chance to lead a normal life. And when the surgery was over, he was going to prove, over and over again, that he loved them both, and wouldn't leave. Not when the going got tough. Not ever.

"I wish Stef would stop being stubborn long enough to imagine how her life could be if this operation is successful," Clarissa whispered on a sigh.

"She's stubborn, all right, but that's part of her charm," he replied.

Kyle watched Clarissa glance up at him, watched her shrug her shoulders and watched as a slow smile crept across her face. Within a few minutes, Mr. Abernathy opened the door. "Ah, Mrs. Cohagan, come in, come in. Stephanie has agreed to have the surgery. She is getting sleepy from her shot, and wants to give you a hug, I think."

Kyle cast an incredulous look from Stephanie, who was resting comfortably against her pillow, to Mr. Abernathy's twinkling blue eyes. Clarissa rushed to her daughter's side, but Kyle hurried after the elderly man who walked faster than any elderly man he'd ever seen.

At the end of the hallway, Kyle caught up with him and the older man turned around. "It is good of you to want to slay Mrs. Cohagan's dragons, Kyle. You are a fine man."

Kyle wondered how the old coot knew about his brother's trophy and latest bet. But he was more curious about something else. "You call me Kyle, yet you always refer to Clarissa as *Mrs. Cohagan.* Why?"

"Because, I'm afraid that in her heart, that is the way Mrs. Cohagan thinks of herself."

Those words sent an ominous sense of foreboding through Kyle, a feeling he would have preferred to attribute to the fact that he hadn't seen the inside of a hospital in more than twenty years. But there was more to this sense of dread than Kyle's dislike of hospitals. Could Mr. Abernathy be right? Could Clarissa still think of herself as a married woman?

Kyle remembered the way she'd felt in his arms, the way she'd reacted to his touch. That hadn't been a married woman in his arms that night in Florida. Mr. Abernathy might have been wonderful with Stephanie, but he was wrong about Clarissa.

The realization eased the crick from Kyle's neck, and eased a portion of his worry about Stef's surgery, too. "What did you say to Stef to change her attitude about this surgery?"

Looking around as if for spies, the old gentleman lowered his voice and rubbed a hand through his white beard before replying. "I simply told her the truth. I explained that her Christmas wish is about to come true."

"What Christmas wish is that?" Kyle asked.

"The wish she made for a father."

Kyle had no idea how the old man could possibly know Stephanie's wish was about to come true, but the idea filled him with hope just the same. If Stephanie got her wish, he'd get his, too.

"Tell me, Kyle. That blue ten-speed bicycle with the silver seat and handlebars was to your liking, yes?"

"The one Uncle Martin left in my driveway on the Fourth of July?"

They'd reached the end of another hall, where Mr. Abernathy pressed the elevator button with the tip of his cane. Kyle narrowed his eyes and said, "It was terrific. How did you know about that bike? Are you a friend of Uncle Martin's?"

"I have many friends, Kyle."

Yes, Kyle thought, the man did have many friends. He'd been a wonderful friend to Stephanie. Feeling less green, less intimidated by the large hospital, Kyle planted his feet a comfortable distance apart. With hands on his hips, he slanted a smile at the old man. "You've always called me Kyle. What do your friends call you?"

The elevator doors slid open and after several people shuffled off, Mr. Abernathy stepped inside then slowly turned to face him. For a long moment, Kyle didn't think the other man was going to answer. When he did, it was in a voice befitting royalty, proud and sure. "My name is Nicholas." The doors began to slide shut. "Nick, to you, yes?"

The old gentleman's deep laughter resounded through the elevator doors, then gradually slid away as the elevator began its slow descent to the ground floor. Kyle's hands slid from his hips just as slowly.

The man's name was Nicholas Abernathy. *Nick? As in St. Nick?* Impossible.

Clarissa stood and paced to the window overlooking a new wing of the huge hospital. Stephanie had been in surgery nearly three hours, and the waiting was wearing on her frayed nerves.

Kyle's relatives had traipsed through the waiting room, offering him their moral support, unconditionally offering it to Clarissa, too. Mitch and Raine, Taylor, their parents, Ed and Mary Harris, even a large-boned woman Kyle introduced as Cousin Trudy, Aunt Millie's daughter, as if that information had significant meaning, came by.

Each one offered them their own brand of comfort, some in the form of a gentle touch and a cup of coffee, others in the form of a slap on the back and a new joke. Clarissa began to fully understand the depth of feeling and commitment these family members harbored toward one another.

They'd stood by one another through thick and thin. The way Kyle was standing by her now.

In a rare moment in which Clarissa and Kyle were alone in the small waiting room, he joined her at the window. In spite of her nerves and her worries, his touch was soothing, his presence endearing.

"She's going to be all right," he whispered, not knowing he was misinterpreting her silence for worry over her daughter.

Yes, she was worried about Stephanie. Clarissa loved that little girl so much her heart ached with it, with the knowledge that, at that very moment, she lay in a sterile room, vulnerable to the surgeon's deft hands.

"Of course she's going to be all right," she murmured. "No matter what the results of this surgery are, she's going to be just fine. Because she's bright and she's strong and she's motivated. She'll go far in this life, Kyle, whether she walks with crutches or without them."

Kyle squeezed her arm, and Clarissa let her head drop to his shoulder, feeling his warmth seep into her cheek and gradually shimmer down her body. She'd thought she could keep their physical relationship separate from the emotional one. Somehow, the two had become tangled, one with the other. From the moment she'd met him, she'd compared him to her father and to Jonathan, silently waiting for him to make a wrong move, subconsciously waiting for him to let her down the way they had.

Kyle hadn't let her down. He'd stood by her, even though he carried his own scars from the past. Even though hospitals scared the living daylights out of him and reminded him of his own shortcomings as a child, he'd waited with her today.

"Any idea how much longer the surgery will take?" Kyle asked.

Clarissa answered with the barest shake of her head. "I'm just glad she finally relaxed and stopped fighting it."

"We can thank Mr. Abernathy for that. You'll never guess what his first name is."

"It begins with an *N*. At least that's what's on his mailbox in the hall. What is it? Norbert? Norton? Nathaniel?"

"Nicholas. Nick. As in St. Nick."

That made her laugh. Kyle always made her laugh. "That's so coincidental, it's eerie," she murmured.

"Know what he said to her to take her mind off her surgery?" Kyle asked.

Clarissa raised her head from his shoulder to gaze up into his eyes, waiting for him to continue. "He told her she was about to have her Christmas wish come true. You remember, the one she told us about on Christmas morning? When she asked for a father for Christmas?"

Both Kyle and Clarissa turned their heads as a noise behind them drew their gazes. A dark-haired, dark-eyed man wearing a scuffed leather bomber jacket and faded jeans stood in the doorway. The man had a strong presence, an unusual aura. The fact that he looked as if he hadn't slept in days did nothing to detract from either.

He walked into the room, each long stride bringing him closer, his dark gaze never wavering from Clarissa's. Stopping beside a row of vinyl chairs, he finally spoke. "Hello, Clarissa. It's been a long time."

"Hello...Jonathan."

Chapter Eleven

Kyle hated hospitals.

He hated their starkness and he hated their smell. Most of all, he hated the fact that his best friend had died in a hospital more than twenty years ago, and he was losing Clarissa in this one today.

She'd come out of her befuddled state and introduced him to Jonathan Cohagan. A tense silence had followed as each man sized up the other. The ensuing conversation had been almost exclusively between Clarissa and Jonathan.

Jonathan told Clarissa he'd seen her and Stephanie on *Good Morning Philadelphia* and went on to explain how he'd practically moved heaven and earth to finish his photography assignment in California to fly here. The man had a brooding quality, and Kyle had been prepared to dislike him. *Dislike* was putting it mildly. But there was something in Jonathan Cohagan's eyes and in his personality: a bit of honesty, a thread of integrity that Kyle couldn't hate, no matter how hard he tried. Evidently, Clarissa couldn't, either.

Kyle studied her face. She listened intently to Jonathan but the expression in her eyes was unreadable. She'd closed herself off. To everyone.

After several terse, tension-filled minutes, Jonathan shrugged in an offhand way and made noises about finding a coffee machine. Kyle had thought the tension in the waiting room had been tangible when Jonathan had arrived. After the man left, it was thick enough to slice.

Kyle was the first to speak. "You going to tell him to get lost?" Unfortunately, the first thing out of his mouth was the last thing he should have said, but Kyle couldn't help it. His patience was wearing thin.

He was afraid Clarissa might break into a million pieces at any moment. Instead of breaking down, she straightened her spine and said, "He's free to leave whenever he wants. And so are you."

"Is that so?"

"Yes. I always thought there was something about Jonathan that reminded me of my father, and something about you that reminded me of Jonathan. Now I know what it is. You're all the carefree bachelor type. Footloose and fancy free."

Kyle felt his blood begin to do a slow boil.

Clarissa's voice had been low, but Kyle felt his climbing nearly to the point of shouting. "I've done everything I can to show you I'm not like your father and ex-husband. But you placed me in a category with them the first time you and I met. And I'm getting sick and tired of being left there."

"I've been honest with you from the beginning."

Her voice hadn't risen as his had, and Kyle found himself at a loss for words. When he finally found his voice, he barely recognized it as his own. "So you're going to let Jonathan waltz back into your life."

"No. He is Stef's father, and if he wants to be in her life he can be. But seeing him again reminded me how hurt I was when he left. It also reminded me why I'm better off on my own."

Kyle wanted to grasp her shoulders and shake her. Or hold on to her for dear life. But sounds near the door drew both heir gazes. Jonathan had entered the room, and the surgeon was right behind him.

"How is she?" Clarissa whispered, rushing to the doctor.

The white-haired surgeon gave her a tired smile. "She's doing very well. Although it's early, I'd say the surgery was a success. I repaired the deformity in both hip joints, and in the muscle in her right leg. She's young and strong. With therapy, I think she'll be able to walk. Who knows, someday she may even run."

Kyle hurried toward the front of the room, ready to take Clarissa in his arms. Jonathan beat him there, swinging her off her feet, letting out a loud whoop for joy.

The sight of the woman he loved in another man's arms froze Kyle's feet to the floor. Blood pounded in his brain, and anger filled the emptiness in the pit of his stomach.

Tears were streaming down Clarissa's cheeks. She disentangled her arms from Jonathan's, and Kyle couldn't label the emotion he saw in the depths of her eyes. Guilt? Embarrassment? He wanted to tell her neither were warranted, certainly neither were what he wanted her to feel for him. Before he could say a word, the surgeon began to speak.

"Your daughter is in the recovery room, but she'll be taken upstairs soon."

"Can I see her?" Clarissa asked.

"Yes," the surgeon replied. Then, turning to Jonathan, he asked, "Are you the child's father?"

Jonathan nodded, and Kyle felt as if he'd been kicked in the stomach.

"If you'll both come with me, I'll explain about your daughter's immediate medical needs."

Clarissa swiped at her cheeks with her fingertips, then slowly turned to Kyle. The expression in her watery eyes touched him in ways he hadn't thought possible. With the

agility and speed of the dancer she'd once been, she turned
and followed the surgeon from the room.

Kyle watched her go. Feeling beaten and utterly deflated,
he watched his dreams go with her.

"Rebound, Kyle!" Taylor sputtered as Mitch stormed to
the basket and won the game.

"Don't yell at me," Kyle groused. "I didn't ask you two
to drag me over here to play basketball in thirty-five-degree
weather."

What he wanted was to be left alone. But his brothers had
never done that. Not when he was a kid, mourning the loss
of his best friend. Not now, when he was a grown man
mourning the loss of his chance to win Clarissa's love.

"You're sure there's no hope for your relationship with
Clarissa?" Mitch asked. "I mean, Raine told me Clarissa
was pretty excited about going to Walt Disney World with
you. And she said Stephanie adores you. Are you sure the
relationship is going nowhere?"

Kyle pounded the pavement with the basketball. To hell
in a hand basket, that's where his and Clarissa's relationship had gone. She'd thrown out warning signals from the
first moment they'd met. He'd stubbornly refused to heed
them. Even Nick Abernathy had seen the shadows in her
eyes for what they really were.

Taylor stole the ball, and draped one arm around Kyle's
shoulders. "Come on inside. It doesn't look like either of us
is going to win that trophy back from Mitch with this latest
bet. At least not tonight at Uncle Martin's party. There may
be damsels out there someplace, but they obviously don't
want to be rescued by us."

Kyle let his brothers lead him inside, let them keep up a
steady stream of idle conversation. He thought about Clarissa and Stephanie all the while. He'd gone to the hospital
earlier this afternoon. Maybe he wasn't Stephanie's father
but he still loved her, still worried about her, still had to see
for himself that she was going to be all right.

Considering it had been only two days since her surgery, the little girl was doing surprisingly well. Her eyes had twinkled when she saw him, and she'd screeched with pleasure when he handed her a brightly wrapped gift.

Kyle had found himself chuckling, his laughter feeling out of place in his own chest. "Where's your mother?" he'd asked as casually as he could manage.

Stephanie cast him a look that spoke of a maturity way beyond her years. She moved her head to one side, motioning toward the door, and said, "She went to the cafeteria. With, you know, with Jonathan, my daddy."

Kyle winced at Stephanie's choice of titles, wishing she would have called Jonathan her *father*. Her *daddy* sounded too much like what Kyle wanted to be.

"Do you suppose I should call him Jonathan, Kyle?"

"I'd say you should ask your mother," Kyle replied.

Stephanie thanked him profusely for the radio he'd given her, and chatted nonstop about the nurses and the other children she'd met in the hospital. She was uncovered, and he'd caught a glimpse of stitches on her upper thigh. He, who couldn't stomach raw eggs and couldn't stand the sight of blood, had found it less difficult than he'd expected not to look away.

Her thin little legs were downright skinny. Without the leg braces, she looked like a bandy-legged cowboy. In a short amount of time, maybe a few weeks, she'd be able to walk without her crutches.

He'd left the hospital without catching a glimpse of Clarissa. Kyle figured it was just as well. He'd always said he was a carefree kind of guy. He'd never claimed to be good at handling complications. And his life was suddenly filled with them. He'd had no business being there. Stephanie wasn't his kid. What did he know about little girls, anyway?

But his biggest complication wasn't Stephanie. His biggest complication was Clarissa. Had been since the day he'd met her.

Kyle had a huge family, in fact had more relatives than he could shake a stick at. He knew they all loved him. But he wanted, needed the love of one lonely woman. Unfortunately, she'd rather go on being lonely than take a chance on trusting him.

That's when it dawned on Kyle. Sure his life had been full of complications since the day he'd met Clarissa. Thinking back, he realized he'd dealt with them pretty well, and he'd had a helluva lot of fun in the process. But unless Clarissa realized she could trust him, nothing else mattered. He couldn't teach her to trust him by himself. She had to work with him to achieve that.

He brought himself from his musings, and tried to follow Mitch and Taylor's conversation. They were talking about Uncle Martin's party, about the reel of film his daughters had transferred to a videocassette tape, a reel of film that featured the girls' only brother. Jason.

Kyle slid his hand into his pocket and bit back a curse. As if the party tonight wouldn't have been difficult enough to get through without that. He figured his spirits couldn't get much lower, and knew there wasn't much he could do about it. There was something wrong with him, something that ached like a physical pain, something no doctor could fix.

He'd gotten through the hospital ordeal, even though it had turned out worse for *him* than he ever would have imagined. Still, he was thankful Stephanie's surgery had been a success. He only hoped he'd get through tonight's party without coming completely unglued.

He told Mitch and Taylor he'd see them tonight, then ambled out to his car. His brothers followed him to the curb, Taylor spouting words of wisdom, words like *there are more fish in the sea,* and *we have only begun to fight,* but Mitch just narrowed his gaze, and kept quiet. Kyle figured Mitch was remembering his own recent courtship with Raine, and how he'd nearly lost her.

Mitch's relationship with Raine had worked out. Kyle now knew his relationship with Clarissa had about a snowball's chance in hell of coming to a similarly satisfying conclusion.

He managed to slip into his car, and managed to start the engine. He didn't lay a patch of rubber pulling away from the curb as he usually did, and wasn't sure why. It was either because he couldn't muster up enough enthusiasm, or because he was saving every last ounce of energy for the party later tonight.

Raine breezed into Stephanie's hospital room like a cyclone. Stephanie clapped her hands, and Clarissa said, "Raine! Why aren't you at the Harris party?"

"I'll tell you in a minute. First, tell me this. Is Jonathan still here?"

It was Stephanie who answered. "He left and I don't think he's coming back for a long time, Auntie Raine. I like him, but he isn't like Kyle."

"Of course he isn't," Raine assured her. "He isn't a Harris."

Clarissa felt her friend's words filter through her, echoing and drifting until they became feelings rather than sounds. *Of course Jonathan isn't like Kyle. Kyle's a Harris.*

Kyle Harris. A man who didn't leave when the going got tough. A man who'd lived through his own heartache, but hadn't let it keep him from loving Stephanie. Or her.

Raine was talking to Stephanie, but Clarissa hardly heard. Her thoughts were churning. Kyle loved her. He'd told her, and shown her, in a hundred different ways. And what had she done? Pushed him away, repeatedly comparing him to Jonathan and her father.

Why hadn't she seen it sooner? Kyle Harris wasn't like either of them. How could he be?

Kyle was one of a kind.

"Raine," she whispered. "Would you mind sitting with Stef for a little while?"

Raine cast her a huge smile. "Why do you think I stopped by?"

Clarissa hurriedly gave Stephanie and Raine a hug then turned and practically ran from the room. Raine caught up with her halfway down the hall. Pulling her to one side, Raine said, "You know how much those Harris men love to give gifts. I thought you might want to give Kyle this."

Raine reached into a paper sack and removed an old, battered trophy. Clarissa tucked the trophy back into the sack and took it from Raine's hands, saying, "Have I told you how lucky I am to have found an assistant like you?"

"As a matter of fact, you have. You and I both know I'm not the only reason you're lucky. Don't you think it's about time you told Kyle? I'll want to hear all about it tomorrow. Now go. If you hurry, you might be able to rescue him from Aunt Millie's clutches."

Chapter Twelve

Clarissa knew something was wrong the second she stepped from her car. It had started to rain, but the weather had nothing to do with her sense of unease. Walking toward the door, she sidestepped a shallow puddle, and glanced around. The parking lot was full of cars, but there was no noise coming from inside the banquet hall. What was going on? The party should have been well under way by now.

Wondering if Raine had somehow given her the wrong address, Clarissa shifted the box she was carrying to her left hand, thinking Raine was too thorough to have made that kind of mistake. With serious misgivings, Clarissa grasped the doorknob, and stepped into the dimly lit room.

"Surprise!" The sudden roar was nearly deafening, the burst of lights blinding.

Clarissa's only consolation was the fact that the party guests looked as surprised as she was. In one motion, she took in the somewhat familiar faces, the shocked expressions.

A high, slightly nasal voice cut the silence from another side of the room. "You're not Martin!"

"You noticed that right away, huh, Aunt Millie?" someone called.

From somewhere came a wolf whistle, followed by a cat-call or two. At least Clarissa knew she was in the right place. This was definitely the Harris party.

Before she could say a word, a breeze cooled her back. Even if she hadn't turned around, Clarissa would have known who was entering the room. Too late, Clarissa realized she'd ruined the surprise.

The man who would turn sixty years old tomorrow, the still-handsome man with gray hair and Harris-blue eyes, cast a sweeping look all around him. "What, somebody throw a party and forget to invite me?" Martin Harris asked in a dramatic baritone.

Someone finally broke the stunned silence and yelled, "Surprise!" A moment later, others picked up the word, still others a moment later, making the word sound like an echo that started in one corner of the room and ended in another.

"Daddy! Where have you been?"

A woman who was probably Martin's wife answered. "We've been stuck along the highway, changing a flat tire, that's where we've been. Honestly, girls, I thought we'd never get here!"

Kyle stood near the center of the room. All around him, he heard noises, his aunts and uncles and cousins calling to one another, jostling and laughing in joviality. Through the roaring din, Kyle remained perfectly still, all his attention focused on the woman wearing the navy blue dress and the enchanting smile.

Mitch suddenly materialized out of the crowd, looping an arm across Kyle's shoulder. "There's your damsel, Kyle. Go on and rescue her from Aunt Millie."

"I should have known you were up to something, Mitch, when you hedged my questions about where Raine had gone."

Mitch laughed, thoroughly enjoying himself, but didn't offer more of an explanation for Raine's whereabouts. Kyle allowed himself to be propelled through the crowd of his relatives, but for the life of him, he didn't know what he'd say to Clarissa once he reached her.

"Goodness gracious," Aunt Millie was spouting. "I should say not! Isn't that right, Kyle?" the short, robust lady asked, turning on him the moment he stepped closer.

When it came to Aunt Millie, Kyle had learned a long time ago that, when in doubt, it was safest to nod. Halfway through the slight movement of his head, he cast a glance at Clarissa, and found her watching him. He saw the warmth and determination in her gaze and in her smile, but didn't know what to make of either of them.

He watched her place a gentle hand on Millie's arm, and heard her say, "The best laid plans of mice and men..." With that, she handed a tall, narrow box to his ample-hipped aunt. "Would you put this with Martin's gifts, Millie?"

"I'd be happy to, dear."

Kyle didn't understand the conspiratorial wink Millie gave Clarissa before setting off for the gift table on the other side of the room. For the life of him, he didn't know why Clarissa had come here.

"Is everything all right with Stef?" he asked.

Clarissa hesitated, measuring him for a moment with her eyes. She found Kyle's nearness disturbing and exciting. There was so much she wanted to tell him, but she was a private person, and wasn't accustomed to confiding her innermost thoughts, especially while standing in the middle of a crowd.

"Stef's fine. Raine offered to stay with her while I came to the party."

Clarissa looked all around her, noticing in one glance all the people with one ear tuned to this conversation. Using Kyle's upper arm for support, she stood on tiptoe to whisper near his ear. "Is there someplace we could go to talk?"

They both looked around, but neither of them found a quiet area uninhabited by members of the Harris family. "Why did you come here tonight?" he asked in that smooth-as-satin voice.

Still on tiptoe, she looked up into Kyle's eyes. Hadn't she always known he was stubborn? He was also loyal, trustworthy and honest. He was a man among men, and even without his sexy voice, he possessed the power to make her heart swell, to make her senses soar. Because of all those things, he deserved an honest answer.

"I came because I finally realized I can trust you, and because, every once in a while, even the bravest and most arrestingly handsome knight needs rescuing."

Lowering her three-inch heels to the floor, Clarissa watched her words temper his expression. He looked as if he were weighing her answer, carefully considering each of her words. After what seemed like an incredibly long time, a probing query glinted in his eyes, and one corner of his mouth lifted, creasing that cheek ever so slightly, just as she remembered.

"You think I'm good-looking?"

Leave it to Kyle to fish for compliments in the middle of the most important declaration of her life. "My new office furniture is good-looking, Kyle. So is the new meteorologist on channel six. You're beyond good-looking. *Way* beyond."

She'd expected him to smile, to spout some trite line. He did neither. More serious than she'd ever seen him, he asked, "Where's Jonathan?"

All around them people were talking. Someone whistled for silence, and the room quickly grew quiet. Through the silence, Clarissa whispered, "He left. Late this afternoon."

A microphone was handed to Martin's oldest daughter, Amelia, who in turn handed her video camera to her husband, and welcomed everyone to her father's party. The lights were dimmed, and a large television was turned on. What followed was a documentary of Martin Harris's life. There were photos of his parents and brothers and sisters, and an old black-and-white film of his and Kathy's wedding thirty-seven years ago.

"I remember that day."

"Oh, he was a handsome devil."

"What do you mean *was?*"

Clarissa had no idea whose comments she heard. She was only aware that she was witnessing a kind of family closeness she'd only read about. Bits and pieces of *do you remember whens* drifted from all over the room.

And then the room grew quiet. On the large-screen TV, a toddler ran across a patch of grass, straight into his mother's arms. Jason Theodore Harris.

Grasping Kyle's hand, Clarissa could feel the tension vibrating through him. He stood so straight, so stiff, she doubted he realized she was there.

The film continued, seconds melting into years as, before their eyes, Jason laughed and played and grew. More often than not, three other little boys shared the film with Jason. Kyle, Mitch and Taylor. Then along came, first one, and then another, little girl—Jason's sisters, Suzie and Amelia. There were sniffles all around, but Clarissa noticed there was laughter, too.

"Look, Suzie," a boisterous cousin called, "I'd recognize those chubby legs anywhere."

"At least I still have hair!" she replied.

There was plenty of conversation, but Clarissa didn't participate. Her gaze had climbed to Kyle's eyes, where the overhead lights glimmering in their depths reminded her of moonlight. She thought of all the times he'd asked her to dance, and all the times she'd turned him down. Kyle hadn't let that stop him. She was beginning to understand a few things about Kyle Harris, and at the same time, about love.

Love was about more than dancing in the moonlight. It was about happiness and sickness, and sometimes sadness. It was about genuine caring, and sticking around when the going gets tough. It was about Kyle. And it was about her.

"You know, Kyle," she whispered, motioning to the television screen. "I wouldn't mind having a little boy who looks just like that. With light blond hair and sky-blue eyes."

Kyle looked toward the screen. "I thought you didn't want any more children."

While everyone else watched Suzie and Amelia grow up, and Martin and Kathy grow older, and searched for glimpses of themselves at parties and family reunions, Kyle led Clarissa toward a shadowed corner, as far away from everyone else in the room as he could get. From the looks he cast at each person he passed, they knew better than to interrupt him. Even Aunt Millie.

He didn't know why Clarissa had come to the party, but he did know that Jonathan Cohagan, with his dark hair and dark eyes, wasn't likely to give her any blond-haired, blue-eyed babies. And Kyle intended to find out what in the hell was going on.

Alone in the crowded room with Kyle, Clarissa didn't know where to begin. After stumbling over three different beginnings, she finally gave up and blurted out the one statement she truly wanted to say. "I came here tonight to tell you I love you."

She watched his expression change from dread to surprise, thinking it felt good to be the one to do the unexpected for a change. "It's true, Kyle. I do love you. I've known it for weeks, but couldn't bring myself to trust my feelings."

"Why?"

"Until this afternoon, I wasn't sure myself. But today, Jonathan and I talked. I learned more about him during that conversation than I knew in the entire three years we were married. He finally told me why he left, why he couldn't face Stephanie. It was because he felt responsible.

"You see, Kyle, I always thought he was an only child. But he had a sister, one born with a debilitating birth defect. His parents didn't deal with it very well, and the girl took her own life when she was sixteen. When Jonathan looked at Stef immediately after her birth, all he could see was the trauma his sister had gone through. For him, the only victory over that kind of pain was flight."

"Then why did he come back?" Kyle asked.

"I think he came back to set us all free. In his own way, he loves Stephanie. But not with the kind of love that withstands pain, and heartache. Not the way you love her, Kyle, the kind of enduring, lasting love filling this room tonight, the kind of love Stef and I feel for you."

Until that moment, Kyle had held himself perfectly still. Backbone straight, he'd somehow managed to keep from touching Clarissa, somehow managed to keep from kissing her. Her declaration changed all that. He took the narrow step separating them, and all in one motion had her in his arms. His head came down, his lips instinctively finding hers.

Her words of love gave the kiss a heady sensation, one that hinted at shared tomorrows, and years of loving, and living. She'd said Jonathan loved Stephanie in his own way. He bet the man loved Clarissa, too. But not with the kind of love that withstood time and distance and even pain. Not the way Kyle loved her.

Long before he wanted the kiss to end, shrill wolf whistles and catcalls and boisterous clapping broke into their idyllic corner. Kyle slowly ended the kiss. Leaving one arm around Clarissa's back, he cast a quick glance from her rosy cheeks to his entire family ogling and cheering them on.

Mitch cut through the group, and gallantly handed Kyle the wrapped package he'd seen Clarissa hand to Aunt Millie shortly after arriving. "What's this?" Kyle asked.

In a quiet voice, Clarissa murmured, "Beware of Harris men bearing gifts."

Mitch's voice was much louder, loud enough to be heard throughout the entire room. "Open it and find out."

Kyle pulled the lid from the box, and extracted their father's old bowling trophy from inside. The guests hooted and laughed, and Mitch waited patiently for them to quiet. "A bet is a bet, Kyle. And you've won this trophy fair and square. But I'd say the real trophy is the love of a good woman, wouldn't you?"

Kyle turned to Clarissa, willing every emotion he felt for this beautiful woman to show in his eyes. Without pulling his gaze from hers, Kyle said, "You're right about the real trophy, Mitch. I'd say you can keep that old bowling trophy. I won't be needing it ever again."

"Oh, this is wonderful," Cousin Trudy declared. "It looks as if there's going to be another wedding in the family."

From nearby, Uncle Martin's voice rang out loud and clear. "So, Taylor, it comes down to you. You're the last in your generation of Harrises to remain single. Tell me, boy, have you tried the grocery store?"

Uncle Joe said, "How about the laundry?"

Aunt Millie sputtered that they'd both lost their minds, and the crowd dispersed, breaking into smaller groups to laugh and reminisce, to talk about shared pasts and current jobs, the children they once were and the children many of them now had. Kyle and Clarissa were swept into the center of the room, where plates of birthday cake were thrust into their hands.

Casting a meaningful look into Clarissa's eyes, Kyle whispered, "Want to get out of here?"

She placed their plates on a table and smiled her answer, as the first sweet notes of a familiar song sounded over a nearby speaker. Kyle cast a quick look toward the door, where Nick Abernathy was making a hasty retreat.

"Is he a friend of yours?" Kyle asked Uncle Martin.

Martin leveled his gaze at Kyle and said, "I've never seen him before in my life. He just whisked in here, handed me that tape, gave me brisk instructions to play it this minute and whisked out again. Looks a lot like Santa Claus, don't you think?"

The other guests laughed. Kyle and Clarissa stared into each other's eyes.

The hand squeezing Kyle's shoulder finally penetrated his consciousness. Martin Harris was normally jovial. Looking into his eyes, Kyle saw that his uncle had grown serious. "I know you've always blamed yourself for Jason's accident, Kyle. But it wasn't your fault. I've always blamed myself for leaving you boys unsupervised, but the truth is it was an accident. Jason slipped. And there wasn't one thing anybody could have done."

"I wish things could have been different, Uncle Martin," Kyle whispered.

Martin nodded in agreement. "A million times I've wished I could go back, keep him from running out onto that diving board. A million times I've wished I would never have put in that swimming pool. But I'll tell you what I've never regretted. I've never regretted having him, if only for twelve short years. And I thank my lucky stars for this whole noisy family."

With a slap on Kyle's back, Martin turned to another relative, and Kyle looked down into Clarissa's eyes.

"He's right, you know," she said softly. "You are lucky to have this crazy, noisy family."

"Look," Taylor called. "The rain is turning to snow."

With a slight smile, Kyle whispered, "Stef always said moonlight on snow brought about a special kind of magic."

Clarissa stepped closer and took his hand in hers. "The snow is outside, but the moonlight has always been in your eyes, Kyle."

The first song had ended, and a second began. Leading him to the small dance floor, she turned to face the man she loved. "Dance with me?"

She felt his arms come around her, and felt him lead h
into the slow, dreamy dance. Around them, others wer
doing the same, couples of all ages slowly swaying to lov
ers' music. She turned her face into Kyle's neck, and smile
as his deep voice quietly murmured the sweet refrain.

"So darlin', save the last dance for me."

From his shoulder she murmured, "From now on, all m
dances are yours, Kyle. All my dances, all my days, and a
my nights."

His voice, that moonlight-and-satin voice, shimmere
close to her ear. "Will you marry me?"

Her answer was a nod, and a kiss, warm and deep an
meaningful. All around them, people danced on, but Cla
rissa's and Kyle's footsteps had stopped. Standing in th
center of the dance floor, heartbeat to heartbeat, a litt
girl's Christmas wish came true.

"Think we should go to the hospital to tell Stef?" h
asked. Her answer was in her eyes. Kyle felt it in his heart

"How soon do you think you could marry me?" h
asked.

With a smile he found sexy as hell, she replied. "It just s
happens that I know an extremely reputable wedding cor
sulting firm. I wouldn't be surprised if they could plan
beautiful wedding in a matter of a few short weeks. Woul
that be soon enough?"

"Tomorrow wouldn't be soon enough. But I guess I ca
wait until then."

With a round of applause and good-natured ribbing, Ky
and Clarissa left a short time later. They hurried through th
doorway, their feet splashing through puddles of rain mixe
with snow. Hand in hand, they stopped and slowly turne
around.

"Did you hear that?" Kyle said softly.

Clarissa nodded, her eyes searching the sky. "It sounde
like sleigh bells."

The sound came again, the sound of sleigh bells tinklin
through the wintry air. "It's magic," Clarissa whispered.

From somewhere bells jingled again, followed by laugher, belly-deep and infectious.

"Mr. Abernathy?" Clarissa called.

"Ho, ho, ho, Nick," Kyle whispered.

"Ho, ho, ho," the voice answered. "And to all a goodnight."

* * * * *

Will Taylor ever win the trophy? Find out how the third Harris brother loses his Wedding Wager in Expectant Bachelor—*coming in January from Silhouette Romance!*

COMING NEXT MONTH

#1048 ANYTHING FOR DANNY—Carla Cassidy

Under the Mistletoe—Fabulous Fathers

Danny Morgan had one wish this Christmas—to reunite his divorced parents. But Sherri and Luke Morgan needed more than their son's hopes to bring them together. They needed to rediscover their long-lost love.

#1049 TO WED AT CHRISTMAS—Helen R. Myers

Under the Mistletoe

Nothing could stop David Shepherd and Harmony Martin from falling in love—though their feuding families struggled to keep them apart. Would it take a miracle to get them married?

#1050 MISS SCROOGE—Toni Collins

Under the Mistletoe

"Bah, humbug" was all lonely Casey Tucker had to say about the holidays. But that was before handsome Gabe Wheeler gave her the most wonderful Christmas gift of all....

#1051 BELIEVING IN MIRACLES—Linda Varner

Under the Mistletoe—Mr. Right, Inc.

Andy Fulbright missed family life, and Honey Truman needed a father for her son. Their convenient marriage fulfilled their common needs, but would love fulfill their dreams?

#1052 A COWBOY FOR CHRISTMAS—Stella Bagwell

Under the Mistletoe

Spending the holidays with cowboy Chance Delacroix was a joy Lucinda Lambert knew couldn't last. She was a woman on the run, and leaving was the only way to keep Chance out of danger.

#1053 SURPRISE PACKAGE—Lynn Bulock

Under the Mistletoe

Miranda Dalton needed a miracle to save A Caring Place shelter. What she got was Jared Tarkett. What could a sexy drifter teach *her* about life, love and commitment?

MILLION DOLLAR SWEEPSTAKES (III)

No purchase necessary. To enter, follow the directions published. Method of entry may vary. For eligibility, entries must be received no later than March 31, 1996. No liability is assumed for printing errors, lost, late or misdirected entries. Odds of winning are determined by the number of eligible entries distributed and received. Prizewinners will be determined no later than June 30, 1996.

Sweepstakes open to residents of the U.S. (except Puerto Rico), Canada, Europe and Taiwan who are 18 years of age or older. All applicable laws and regulations apply. Sweepstakes offer void wherever prohibited by law. Values of all prizes are in U.S. currency. This sweepstakes is presented by Torstar Corp., its subsidiaries and affiliates, in conjunction with book, merchandise and/or product offerings. For a copy of the Official Rules send a self-addressed, stamped envelope (WA residents need not affix return postage) to: MILLION DOLLAR SWEEPSTAKES (III) Rules, P.O. Box 4573, Blair, NE 68009, USA.

EXTRA BONUS PRIZE DRAWING

No purchase necessary. The Extra Bonus Prize will be awarded in a random drawing to be conducted no later than 5/30/96 from among all entries received. To qualify, entries must be received by 3/31/96 and comply with published directions. Drawing open to residents of the U.S. (except Puerto Rico), Canada, Europe and Taiwan who are 18 years of age or older. All applicable laws and regulations apply; offer void wherever prohibited by law. Odds of winning are dependent upon number of eligibile entries received. Prize is valued in U.S. currency. The offer is presented by Torstar Corp., its subsidiaries and affiliates in conjunction with book, merchandise and/or product offering. For a copy of the Official Rules governing this sweepstakes, send a self-addressed, stamped envelope (WA residents need not affix return postage) to: Extra Bonus Prize Drawing Rules, P.O. Box 4590, Blair, NE 68009, USA.

SWP-S1194

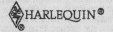 

"HOORAY FOR HOLLYWOOD" SWEEPSTAKES

HERE'S HOW THE SWEEPSTAKES WORKS

OFFICIAL RULES — NO PURCHASE NECESSARY

To enter, complete an Official Entry Form or hand print on a 3" x 5" card the words "HOORAY FOR HOLLYWOOD", your name and address and mail your entry in the pre-addressed envelope (if provided) or to: "Hooray for Hollywood" Sweepstakes, P.O. Box 9076, Buffalo, NY 14269-9076 or "Hooray for Hollywood" Sweepstakes, P.O. Box 637, Fort Erie, Ontario L2A 5X3. Entries must be sent via First Class Mail and be received no later than 12/31/94. No liability is assumed for lost, late or misdirected mail.

Winners will be selected in random drawings to be conducted no later than January 31, 1995 from all eligible entries received.

Grand Prize: A 7-day/6-night trip for 2 to Los Angeles, CA including round trip air transportation from commercial airport nearest winner's residence, accommodations at the Regent Beverly Wilshire Hotel, free rental car, and $1,000 spending money. (Approximate prize value which will vary dependent upon winner's residence: $5,400.00 U.S.); 500 Second Prizes: A pair of "Hollywood Star" sunglasses (prize value: $9.95 U.S. each). Winner selection is under the supervision of D.L. Blair, Inc., an independent judging organization, whose decisions are final. Grand Prize travelers must sign and return a release of liability prior to traveling. Trip must be taken by 2/1/96 and is subject to airline schedules and accommodations availability.

Sweepstakes offer is open to residents of the U.S. (except Puerto Rico) and Canada who are 18 years of age or older, except employees and immediate family members of Harlequin Enterprises, Ltd., its affiliates, subsidiaries, and all agencies, entities or persons connected with the use, marketing or conduct of this sweepstakes. All federal, state, provincial, municipal and local laws apply. Offer void wherever prohibited by law. Taxes and/or duties are the sole responsibility of the winners. Any litigation within the province of Quebec respecting the conduct and awarding of prizes may be submitted to the Regie des loteries et courses du Quebec. All prizes will be awarded; winners will be notified by mail. No substitution of prizes are permitted. Odds of winning are dependent upon the number of eligible entries received.

Potential grand prize winner must sign and return an Affidavit of Eligibility within 30 days of notification. In the event of non-compliance within this time period, prize may be awarded to an alternate winner. Prize notification returned as undeliverable may result in the awarding of prize to an alternate winner. By acceptance of their prize, winners consent to use of their names, photographs, or likenesses for purpose of advertising, trade and promotion on behalf of Harlequin Enterprises, Ltd., without further compensation unless prohibited by law. A Canadian winner must correctly answer an arithmetical skill-testing question in order to be awarded the prize.

For a list of winners (available after 2/28/95), send a separate stamped, self-addressed envelope to: Hooray for Hollywood Sweepstakes 3252 Winners, P.O. Box 4200, Blair, NE 68009.

CBSRLS

OFFICIAL ENTRY COUPON

"Hooray for Hollywood"
SWEEPSTAKES!

Yes, I'd love to win the Grand Prize — a vacation in Hollywood —
or one of 500 pairs of "sunglasses of the stars"! Please enter me
in the sweepstakes!

This entry must be received by December 31, 1994.
Winners will be notified by January 31, 1995.

Name _____

Address _____ Apt. _____

City _____

State/Prov. _____ Zip/Postal Code _____

Daytime phone number _____
(area code)

Mail all entries to: Hooray for Hollywood Sweepstakes,
P.O. Box 9076, Buffalo, NY 14269-9076.
In Canada, mail to: Hooray for Hollywood Sweepstakes,
P.O. Box 637, Fort Erie, ON L2A 5X3.

KCH

OFFICIAL ENTRY COUPON

"Hooray for Hollywood"
SWEEPSTAKES!

Yes, I'd love to win the Grand Prize — a vacation in Hollywood —
or one of 500 pairs of "sunglasses of the stars"! Please enter me
in the sweepstakes!

This entry must be received by December 31, 1994.
Winners will be notified by January 31, 1995.

Name _____

Address _____ Apt. _____

City _____

State/Prov. _____ Zip/Postal Code _____

Daytime phone number _____
(area code)

Mail all entries to: Hooray for Hollywood Sweepstakes,
P.O. Box 9076, Buffalo, NY 14269-9076.
In Canada, mail to: Hooray for Hollywood Sweepstakes,
P.O. Box 637, Fort Erie, ON L2A 5X3.

KCH